CANYON: LIFE IS A GAMBLE

ALSO BY MONTY R. GARNER

Buckshot

Card Jordan Series

Card, Kill Them All

Card, Man of Justice

Card, Taking Care of Business

Card, Day of Reckoning

Card, Duty Calls

Card, Unleashed

Card, A Test of Faith

CANYON: LIFE IS A GAMBLE

MONTY R. GARNER

WOLFPACK
PUBLISHING
— EST 2013 —

Canyon: Life Is a Gamble
Paperback Edition
Copyright © 2025 (As Revised) by Monty R. Garner

Wolfpack Publishing
1707 E. Diana Street
Tampa, FL 33610

www.wolfpackpublishing.com

Paperback ISBN 979-8-89567-796-4
Ebook ISBN 979-8-89567-795-7

CANYON: LIFE IS A GAMBLE

CHAPTER ONE

A fly buzzed around the gambler's face and landed on his forehead. He never changed his expression or swatted at the insect. Instead, he sat in his chair with his eyes moving from player to player as they decided to continue to play or fold. Years of practice had shaped him into a man capable of showing no facial expressions, never letting anyone see what he was thinking, or divulging whether it was a good or bad hand. Five cards lay on the table in front of him, face down, while he waited for the man to his immediate left to decide what to do.

Oliver Canyon Golden, riverboat gambler, gunfighter, and drifter, sat patiently, but it was time for him to speed up the game so he could make his play. He took the forefinger of his right hand and tapped the top of the card table. This was something he had learned from an older player on one of the riverboats. The habitual tapping was done in time to an imaginary tune. The intimidating noise aggravated the other players and took their minds off their cards so they couldn't concentrate on the hands they'd been dealt.

It was hot from the afternoon heat on a July day in 1876. Inside the dim saloon in Albany, Texas, the patrons drinking and the ones sitting at the poker tables playing cards didn't let the sweat beading on their faces give away what cards they were holding. The man to Oliver's left, Lilburn McFarlan, the local hardware store owner, picked up a few dollar bills and dropped them on top of the small pile of money on the table.

"I bet five dollars and need three cards." He flipped the rejected cards onto the table.

The man across from Oliver, Raymond, was also the dealer and a sizable overweight man who kept wiping the sweat from his hands with a bar rag before dealing the cards. He took a deep breath and threw two cards into the pile and said, "I'll see your five dollars and take two cards."

The man to Oliver's right placed his money on the table. "I want four cards." His name was Sonny Wilson, and he owned the freight wagon business. He was a short man with a barrel chest, huge arms, and wide shoulders from loading and unloading freight.

Oliver knew from the way that Sonny's hands shook and the way he kept looking from one player to the next that he didn't have anything. Oliver stopped tapping his finger on the table, picked up a single bill, and flipped it on top of the money in the center of the table. He then picked up some more greenbacks. "I see your five dollars and raise you fifteen more. Deal me two cards." He pushed the money toward the pile and began tapping his finger again.

Each of the three other players put in their bets, and the dealer gave them their requested number of cards. Oliver cupped the two cards that were dealt to him in his hands so no one could see what he had. It was a pair of kings to go along with his two nines. He lay the cards on the table and tapped his finger again.

The man to his left took his sweet time looking at his cards before he finally said, "I check." Oliver knew the man wasn't holding a pat hand. Lilburn had a habit of breathing in through his mouth when he had a good hand, and that wasn't happening now.

The dealer laid twenty dollars on the table. "I bet twenty." He picked up his rag and dried his hands again. Oliver knew he was bluffing because his face was sweating profusely, and it wasn't from just the heat.

Sonny Wilson folded and drank warm beer from the mug sitting to his right. Oliver picked up his money and put two more twenties in the pot. "I see your twenty and raise you twenty."

Then he returned to his intentionally annoying habit and tapped his finger gently on the table. The other two players put in their money, and Oliver turned his cards over to show his two pairs of kings and nines.

Lilburn threw his cards into the pile without showing what he had. "I can't beat that."

Raymond put his on top of the deck and picked up the rest of the cards to start shuffling them for the next hand. "Good hand, mister. By the way, what's your name?"

"I go by Ollie." Oliver reached across the table and pulled his winnings into a pile in front of him, adding the bills to his stack.

Three men came abruptly through the saloon door. The one in the lead was dressed much nicer than the other two, wearing a new black hat, gray britches, and a black shirt with a string necktie.

They made loud remarks to the barkeeper and the girls waiting tables. "Get one of your hussies over to our table. We want drinks," said one of the cowboys.

The well-dressed man pointed to one of the girls and said, "Elizabeth, come and take our order now!"

Lilburn said in a quiet voice that only the players at the table could hear, "Jeff and his cronies just came in."

Oliver watched them start across the room, but Raymond and Sonny had yet to look at the newcomers. It seemed to Oliver that they didn't want to have any eye contact with the men.

That was a common thing in saloons and gambling halls. Bad men wanted to make trouble, and the good citizens would keep their heads down or turn away before they had a confrontation and someone got hurt.

The room became quiet as the men pushed a few patrons out of their path.

"Move out of the way. We're coming through," said a man who looked to be a cowpuncher, wearing a sweaty hat and dirty britches with the legs of his pants tucked inside his boots. The three men sauntered across the room like they owned the place. The man wearing black stopped in front of the table next to the poker game where a gentleman sat drinking a beer. The other two men stopped behind him and one of them bumped into the back of Lilburn, but Lilburn didn't say anything.

"Mister, you're at my table and it's time for you to leave, or my men will make you wish you were never born," said the man in black.

"Yeah, that's right," said the cowboy as he walked to the gentleman's chair and grabbed him by the arm.

"You don't have to be rough, Mr. Jeff. I'm going to leave."

"Then get going and stop jawing," said Jeff, who slapped the man across the face. The two men with Jeff grabbed hold of the gentleman's arms, dragged him away from the table and dropped him on the floor. One of the men stomped him in the back as he lay face down on the saloon floor.

"Let this be a lesson to any of you that gets in my way," warned Jeff.

The other two started back to the table and as they went by people sitting at other tables, they would knock off their hat or slap them on the back of their head, all the time cursing at them.

Oliver ignored their obnoxious behavior and loud outbursts as they sat down. He finished stacking his money while the cards were shuffled and the dealer began dealing a new hand.

Oliver could tell the well-dressed man was in charge by his abusive language and mannerisms, and that the other two were along for the ride. "You two need to take a bath and change clothes," said Jeff. "Both of you stink, and I don't want it rubbing off on me. My father would make you leave the saloon if he was here."

What stuck out the most about his appearance was the two-gun rig he wore slung around his hips and the tie-down holsters fastened to his legs with rawhide. He must have been fast on the draw with the two pearl-handled pistols.

Every time he spoke, his words were loud and sarcastic. "Where's my whiskey?" Jeff demanded in a loud voice. "I'm getting tired of having to wait on these lazy girls." The other two men chimed in and went along with his remarks.

The server came to their table with a bottle and three glasses. As she set the bottle down, the man called Jeff put his arm around her waist and tried to hug her. "Hello, Elizabeth. How about some sugar?" The waitress jerked away from him, and the glasses she'd been holding hit the floor.

Jeff laughed, but then got earnest, and an expression of rage lit up his face. He put his finger in the frightened girl's face and said, "You pick them glasses up and go fetch us clean ones. Now get going!" The girl picked up the glasses and started off. Jeff turned to his friends and laughed before pulling the cork from the bottle and taking a swig of the whiskey inside.

"Jeff, I think she likes you," said one of the other men.

"Yeah, I think I'll get me some sugar when she returns," said Jeff.

Oliver tried to ignore the men at the other table and keep his mind on his cards, but that was hard to do. When Elizabeth returned with three clean glasses, Oliver had picked up some bills and was about to make a bet.

She bent over the table to set the shot glasses down, and Jeff leaned over and kissed her on the left cheek. "You like that, baby?" he asked.

Her right hand came around and she hit him on the jaw with her open hand, which made a sound that caught most of the crowd's attention. Oliver dropped the money back onto the tabletop and scooted his chair away from the table.

Jeff jumped up from his chair, grabbed the girl's throat with his left hand, and brought his right hand up to hit her, but Oliver quickly rose from his seat, took two steps, and grabbed Jeff's arm.

"Not today, mister. We don't hit ladies where I come from," he said. Jeff turned her throat loose and threw a left hook at Oliver's head. Oliver raised up his arm and blocked the punch. With his other hand, he hit Jeff square in the nose.

Blood ran down and over the man's top lip, and he took his sleeve and wiped it off. "I'll kill you for that, mister!" Jeff tried to backhand the gambler.

Oliver ducked the punch and hit Jeff with a left cross

that knocked the man to the floor. "You need to stay down and apologize to the lady," he said.

The other two men were so surprised by seeing their boss get whipped that it took them a few seconds to go to his aid and help him up.

Oliver turned to go back to his poker game and heard Jeff say, "Don't you turn your back on me! I'll kill you right here for hitting me, so turn around."

Oliver looked at the men sitting at the poker table, who were shaking their heads in a negative way and trying to move away from the fight.

The gambler's shoulders dropped. *Here we go again. Some overconfident spoiled brat wants to draw on me.*

He pulled his coattail to the rear of his gun and tucked it into the back of his britches. Oliver turned toward the overconfident bully, standing with his hands close to his guns. The gambler tapped his index finger against the holster. "You still have time to turn and walk away," he said, his face showing the same cold, emotionless expression that he used when playing cards.

Jeff spat blood on the floor and went for his gun. Oliver palmed his weapon in his hand and was firing before Jeff ever got off a shot. The gunfighter received three slugs in his chest, took two steps backward, and fell to the ground. Oliver turned his gun to Jeff's two thugs. They both threw up their hands to take themselves out of the action.

"Don't shoot, mister. We ain't goin' to pull iron," said one of the men.

"Lay your pistols on the floor really easy and don't make any fast moves," said Oliver.

"Mister, we ain't in this fight, so don't you get any ideas when we take our guns out of our holsters," said the man who had his britches legs tucked into his boots.

Both men placed their guns on the floor as directed.

Oliver opened the cylinder on his pistol, ejected the three spent shells, and reloaded, still standing in the same spot and watching the two men. One of them was trying to check if his friend had a heartbeat, while the other one was swatting at flies trying to get to the blood that was pooling around Jeff's body.

Oliver backed up enough to lean over and get his money off the table. "Playing poker with you fellers was fun, but it's probably time for me to leave."

Sonny looked at him. "You don't know who that is you just killed, do you?"

"No. Should I?"

"That's Jeff Gaines. His daddy is Paul Gaines, and I guarantee he will ride to the ends of the earth to kill you."

"The name, Paul Gaines, doesn't resonate with me. But if anyone wants to come find me, you can tell him that Oliver Golden will be waiting."

"Well, that explains why you took Jeff so easy. The infamous Oliver Golden was here playing poker with us! Good luck, Oliver, you'll need it. Paul has a crew of gun hands on his payroll," said Lilburn.

"Thanks for the advice," Oliver said, easing his way toward the door so he could make sure the other two men didn't shoot him in the back. He was almost to the stairs that led to the second floor when the town marshal entered the saloon. Oliver stopped and waited until the marshal saw the corpse on the floor. Then he turned to the gambler standing by the stairs. "Did you kill Jeff?"

"I did. Jeff pulled on me, and I shot him in self-defense. You can ask anyone here, and they'll tell you he drew first," said Oliver as he motioned toward the men and women in the room.

"That ain't goin' to matter when his pa finds out you killed his boy. What's your name?"

"I'm Oliver Golden."

"Mister Golden, I suggest you get as far away from here as possible and don't go west."

"Thanks, Marshal. I'll be on my way."

CHAPTER TWO

Oliver hurriedly climbed the stairs to the second floor, taking two treads at a time. He wanted to change into his traveling clothes and get his bag from his rented room. He also had a room at the hotel on the east side of town, but had been staying at the saloon, which was on the west side of town, the last couple of days so he could be close to the poker games.

Once inside the room, he removed the shoulder holster that he wore under his coat. Next he pulled off his fancy clothes that he wore while gambling—a waist-length dress jacket, a nice linen shirt, and wool pants.

He changed into his striped wool pants, pulled a plain linen shirt over his head and tucked it into the waist of his pants. He put on his felt cowboy hat so he'd blend in with the locals and the country folks.

With the gambling clothes folded and placed in his travel bag, he put his shoulder holster rig back on and covered it with a cowhide vest he had bought somewhere along his travels. Out of habit, he removed the gun and checked the cylinders to make sure they were fully loaded. For some reason, he took a moment to sit on the edge of the bed and recall what had happened in the saloon, considering his next move. He had to stop getting himself into situations that involved gunplay. Someday he would face someone faster than him.

If Paul Gaines was as persistent in hunting him down as the man's reputation suggested, Oliver decided he wanted to know what he was up against.

After easing the door open enough to look up and down the hallway, he exited the room and walked to the closed door that connected the hallway to the outside stairway. Taking the alleyway south until he came to a side street would keep him partially hidden from the town's citizens. With his hat pulled low to cover his face as much as possible, he went to the livery stable on the west side of town where his horse was stabled.

The man at the livery met him at the door. "Howdy, mister, I have your horse saddled in the second stall."

Oliver gave him a questioning look. "Why did you saddle my horse?"

"I figured you'd be heading out of town quickly after what happened at the saloon," said the barn hustler. "I know I would be if Paul Gaines was coming for me. I left your packhorse in the corral because I figured you wouldn't want to be slowed down by him."

"Thanks, I appreciate you doing that. What will you give me for the packhorse and saddle?"

"I'll give you sixty for everything."

"Pay me. I'm going to take a few of my things off the pack saddle before I head out."

"That's fine by me. You get whatever you need."

Oliver took out a skillet, a coffeepot, a small sack of coffee, some beef jerky, and two cans of beans. That would be sufficient until he could get to another town.

The man walked over to Oliver, who had his things laid out on a bale of hay. "Here's a flour sack that you can use for your stuff. I hope you know where you're going when you leave here."

"I've been told to ride in any direction except west. So how far north do I need to ride until I can turn west again?" asked Oliver.

The man stood thinking for a few seconds. "Mr. Gaines operates on a lot of range land west of here. I'd probably go north at least fifty miles before I turn west. His hacienda is located eight west and six north."

"Hacienda? Should I assume that's where his hired guns also stay?"

"Yep. Mister, you need to get goin' and never come back here. Paul Gaines is mean to the core and has no quit in him."

"Thanks. I best be on my way."

Oliver left the stable and headed north out of Albany, Texas, at a lope. Every so often, he would look back toward town until the shapes of the buildings were out of sight. About thirty minutes later he turned toward the east and circled back toward town, but entered from the east and went to the nearest livery stable to host his horse. He figured that if Gaines lived west of town, they would inquire about him at the livery stable he just left.

The hotel where he rented a room was also on the east side of the city. After leaving the livery, he entered the hotel through the back door. He stayed hidden in the hallway near the lobby until the clerk had his back to him. Then Oliver acted quickly and went up the stairs to his room.

If he figured right, one of the men who had been with Jeff had already ridden to the Gaines Ranch to let his boss know that his son was dead. That meant the men from the Gaines Ranch should be coming into town soon to collect Jeff's corpse. Oliver sat at the window so he could see the men when they came into town. The undertaker's parlor was almost due north across the street from him, and he hoped he could get a good look at Paul Gaines and his gun hands.

Oliver had been in similar situations before, so he understood that the more he knew about the men hunting him, the better. He might even know some of the men since he had been traveling from town to town the last few years. Gun hands and gamblers seemed to have a few things in common, like saloons and drinking. He had met some bad men over the years who hired on to whoever paid the most wages and it seemed that when they weren't working, they were drinking away the memories of who they were or what they had done.

With his chair situated close to the window so he could watch the street, he figured that he still had time to make sure what little belongings he had in the room were packed and ready. That way, he could leave in a hurry. Men hated to wait on others; they wanted to be in control. The waiting game was not new to Oliver. He knew that when he was sitting at a poker table he was always in control, but his opponents didn't usually realize it. He was always careful and methodical in how he forced an opponent to offer a bet or make a play on his cards. The one important thing he had learned early in his career was that men like to blame someone else for their lack of poker skills. And that usually meant gunplay.

Be patient, get comfortable and wait until Paul Gaines and his men came to town, he told himself. Patience was a virtue that a gambler had to practice so he wouldn't give away what cards he was holding. At this critical point in time, Oliver needed to know what and who he was going to be up against before he bet his next hand.

It would get dark soon, and he hoped the men would arrive while it was still light enough for him to see them from the hotel window. If it was too dark to see by the time they showed up, he would have to get as close as he could to them without giving away who he was. But for now, all he had to do was wait or maybe take a short nap.

Forty minutes later, Oliver stood up at the window and looked to the west. A group of horsemen rode into town and stopped in front of the saloon. Two riders dismounted and went inside while the rest sat on their mounts. Oliver counted eight men total, but none looked to be Paul Gaines. He assumed that Paul would at least be middle-aged, and all these riders were considerably younger.

After ten minutes, the two men returned to the group and they walked their horses down the street toward the undertaker's parlor. Oliver eased away from the window so he couldn't be seen from the road.

The riders spread out on both sides of the street like they were there to guard someone or something. One of the men who had gone into the saloon dismounted from a black horse with a white splotch on his right hindquarter, and the others followed his move. The man wore his gun low on his hip, the holster tied to his leg. He kept his gun hand free and used his left hand to tie his horse to the hitching post. This was most likely the top hired gun, possibly the foreman at the ranch.

Oliver looked at each man and tried to study their movements to see what he could figure out about them as individuals. The last man he scrutinized got his attention as someone to always be aware of. Petite in stature and skinny, with a narrow, chiseled face, this particular man stood off to himself and kept looking up and down the street while smoking a hand-rolled cigarette. The others began to bunch up and talk, but this man seemed like a loner who didn't miss anything around him. Oliver watched the narrow-faced man throw down his cigarette butt and start rolling another one. He made a mental note that if he ever tangled with that bunch, he'd kill this man first.

Soon, another group of five riders came down the street, and this time Oliver didn't have to wonder who was in charge. Paul Gaines sat tall in the saddle, wearing a suit that didn't belong in Texas. He was a large man, and when he dismounted, he towered over the men around him. He must have been close to six foot seven, with broad shoulders. His suit had probably been shipped in from one of the big cities back east.

Next, a buckboard wagon pulled up with two men riding in the spring seat. Paul said something and motioned for some of the other men to follow him inside as he entered the mortician's office. A moment later he came out first, followed by several men carrying a wooden coffin. Paul stood by the wagon's side, pointing and talking while his hired hands placed the simple wooden box made out of rough sawed lumber in the back and secured it with rope.

Paul climbed back into the saddle and rode in front of the wagon while the four riders who had come with him brought up the rear.

As he passed by the gunhand who Oliver thought was in charge, Paul stopped long enough to say something to the man, most likely giving him instructions out of hurt and anger. The suspected foreman motioned with a quick gesture of his left hand to the rest of the group, and they all mounted up and followed the wagon until they got to the livery stable on the west side of town where Oliver had originally kept his horse and sold the man his pack animal only hours earlier.

The eight riders pulled up in front of the livery, and Oliver could see the hustler point north as he talked to the leader of the men. Oliver smiled. His plan had worked, and soon the riders would be on a wild goose chase to the north.

CHAPTER THREE

Oliver Canyon Golden grew up in Saint Louis, Missouri. He was the only child of Rebecca and Horatio Golden. His pa worked on the shipping docks as a foreman and made enough money to support his family. Rebecca was a stay-at-home wife and mother who made Oliver go to school even after he started to work.

At fifteen, Oliver took his first real job as a custodian on the General Lee Riverboat while it was docked in the harbor. It was hard, nasty work keeping the floors clean, especially when the wealthy and privileged spit tobacco juice and dropped cigarette butts, food and drink trash for the hired help to clean up. His parents tried to make him quit and spend more time studying his school lessons, but he was infatuated with the gamblers, especially the card players. He only cared about studying arithmetic in school because he learned that odds and percentages were significant factors in winning games of chance.

Oliver spent every free minute watching the men play poker and then would practice shuffling and dealing cards for hours at home. Every time his mother found his cards, she would throw them in the trash and scold him about the sins of gambling.

Often when he would make his way into the poker rooms to watch, the pit bosses would run him off or keep him from watching the action up close. However, he was learning to count cards anyway, and knew he would have the advantage over other players when the time came for him to play. The other important thing he picked up was never to show facial expressions when looking at your cards.

One night between his sixteenth and seventeenth birthday, right before he started his shift on a Saturday night, Oliver met an elderly man who was getting some fresh air outside the poker room, and they started a conversation as they stood next to the railing. His name was Beauregard Lasalle, and Oliver had watched him play cards and other games of chance on many occasions.

Beauregard was leaning against the rail when Oliver walked by on his way to fetch his broom and mop. "Boy, what's your name?" asked the gambler.

"It's Oliver, sir. You're an outstanding poker player."

"What makes someone a good poker player?" Beauregard asked.

"You win a lot of hands, and I never know what you're holding. You don't show any emotions when you look at your cards."

"I see. Do you pay attention to the other players' faces when they look at their cards?"

"Oh, yes sir. Most players don't express any emotions at all."

"You're not really watching what they do. For instance, if Colonel Fred gets a good hand, he squirms in his chair. Alexander Robar will lick his lips. You not only have to watch their facial expressions, but also their body language."

"I hadn't been watching for that. I've only been studying the players' faces and eyes," said Oliver.

"I've been studying you also, Oliver. When you're observing the game and whoever you're watching gets a good hand, you tap your index finger against your leg. That's a dead giveaway that they've got a good hand."

"I didn't realize that I did that. I'm surprised the pit boss hasn't seen it and kicked me out for watching."

"You must learn how to control it. Do you plan on becoming a gambler or a dealer in the future? If you do, you can use that as your calling card to intimidate the other players. Think about this when you look at your cards and place them on the table. You can tap that finger on the table to disrupt the other players. Those are things that a good gambler will learn over time."

"I appreciate you talking to me. But I have to get busy. It's time for me to start work, and I don't want to get in trouble with my boss. He doesn't like me spending my time learning cards."

Beauregard turned and patted Oliver on the back as the boy started off to work. "You keep practicing and watching. It will help you as you mature into a real player."

After that night, Oliver studied each player and practiced picking up on their body language.

The riverboats had gotten to where they would load up at the docks and then put out onto the river and go downstream a ways. After so many hours, the boat would turn around and come back to harbor and let off most of their passengers. This was especially true for people who had jobs in the city and couldn't afford to be gone for days.

When he was almost eighteen, he spent days asking the pit boss to let him fill in as a dealer on the nights they were short-handed. The boss finally gave the young man his big chance and let him work the small stakes table when he needed an extra dealer. Oliver became an excellent dealer and saved up his wages and tips. After that, he wanted to be a gambler and play cards.

Five days before his nineteenth birthday, his ma became very sick. On the third day of her suffering, Oliver was sitting by her bedside when she reached out and took his hand. "Ollie," she said, as that was what she called him. "Last night a visitor stood at the foot of my bed."

"What are you talking about?" asked Oliver with a confused look.

"Listen to what I'm telling you. The visitor wore a black robe with a hood on his head. I couldn't see his face. I initially thought he was a priest coming to pray for me. But now that I've had time to think about it, it was the death angel coming to watch me before he takes me to heaven. Ollie, I love you and want you to promise me you'll take care of your pa when I'm gone."

"Mama, stop it. You're not going anywhere," said Oliver, tears rolling down his cheeks.

"Listen to me. I'm prepared to go meet my maker. I regret that I won't see you grown or married with kids. But Ollie, I'll be gone in the morning, and I want you to stay with me tonight."

"Mama, I'll be here with you, I promise."

Oliver stayed by his mama's bedside and drifted off to sleep sometime during the night. When he woke up, his ma had her eyes closed and a slight smile on her face. He tried to wake her, but she was gone. The heartbroken boy went out of the room and woke up his pa.

The next three days were a blur; he was sad and heartbroken over his ma, but having to comfort his pa and help make funeral arrangements just made it worse.

A week after her funeral, Oliver started playing cards

in the local taverns when he wasn't working on one of the steamboats. However, he still needed to improve his card dealing skills to be chosen to go with the boat when it steamed to New Orleans. After many conversations with the main pit boss, the young gambler volunteered to be on standby in the poker room in case one of the regular dealers didn't show up for work. The only problem he thought he might have was the calluses on his hands from all the sweeping and mopping he did. They made it difficult for him to feel the edges of the cards for nicks or scratches. He had been taught by a few of the regular dealers, who had given him pointers to feel along the edges of the cards for marks made by some players who tried for an advantage over the other players. The riverboats did everything they could to stop cheating at cards, but sometimes they couldn't catch everyone.

His pa started to drink heavily after the death of his beloved Rebecca. Many nights Oliver would come home from work to find him passed out on the couch. Then, three months after his mama's death, Horatio was in a fatal accident at the wharf.

Young Oliver endured the agony of making funeral arrangements and burying his other parent. After the funeral, he spent even more time playing poker in pickup games around town.

He began to win more than he lost, and one night after winning over three hundred dollars in a pickup game at a saloon, the realities of greed and crime that his mama had warned him about were made known in a tangible way. As the young gambler walked home that night, filled with pride about winning so much money, two men accosted him on the street by pulling a gun on him and demanding his winnings. Of course he obliged the men and gave them what they wanted. They took his money, hit him on the side of his head with a club about one foot long. As he lay in the street, they hit and kicked him before leaving with his winnings.

The next day he took his life savings to the gun shop and spent part of his money on a shoulder holster and gun. When it was getting dark, he went back to the same tavern as the night before and played poker, hoping the two men who robbed him would be there. Again he won money, and about a half block away from the tavern on his way home, he spotted two men following him. He went ahead and removed the gun from its holster, ready and waiting when the men caught up to him.

"Hold up, kid, we want to talk to you," said one of the men.

Oliver kept walking and didn't acknowledge the command.

One of the men grabbed Oliver by the back of his jacket, but Oliver turned around and fired his gun. The would-be assailant fell to the ground, mortally wounded. Oliver turned the barrel on the other man and fired two bullets into his chest.

The young gambler stood, shaking in disbelief. He had just killed two men. He took deep breaths, put the gun back into the holster, and kneeled to look at the two men in the dim light. They were the two men from the night before, so he went through their pockets and removed what money they had on them.

Oliver walked away from the corpses, and at the corner he turned onto a dark street and ran the rest of the way to his house.

It was his first bad experience that came with gambling. He later learned that a man also had to protect himself during a game, not just after one. One night when he was lucky and winning hands, one of the players called him a cheat and stood up to pull his gun.

Oliver quickly reacted by pulling his gun first and killing the man. After that incident, he started to get a reputation for being a gambling gun hand.

It was only a short time before his status as a good gambler, and one that was capable of winning the big pots, got around to the local taverns. Buying a seat at the tables became difficult because the amateur players didn't want him in their games. He had to start making arrangements with the men who ran the high-stakes games that featured the more experienced players, and the buy-ins for those games was much more significant. He almost went broke before he began to win some games.

When he started to win at the high-stakes establishments, he quit his job on the river boats and tried to play poker every night. The money he made was what kept him going. He had dreams and he needed money to develop his future.

At the ripe age of twenty-one, his skills at the poker table had developed, and he had put together a substantial nest egg. His goal was to book a cabin on the riverboat and take it to New Orleans so he could gamble with the wealthy patrons on the journey there during cotton harvest when men would have lots of money from the sale of their crops. He had been told that November was the best time to cash in on the big games in Memphis and other shipping ports along the Mississippi River.

The money from the sale of his family home was added to his gambling funds in October so he could get in on the high-stakes games once he was on the boat.

Oliver had matured quite well, standing six foot two, and a lean two hundred pounds. He kept himself groomed by shaving and keeping his brown hair cut at least once every two weeks. He was a gambler, and his appearance was important to him. He had his everyday clothes and fancier clothes which consisted of wool slacks, a linen shirt and dress jacket to hide his gun.

He spent a considerable amount of time dressed in his gaming clothes just sitting in front of a mirror watching himself. He watched his blue eyes for any indication of weakness or strength. A man's facial expressions always told a story, and he practiced so that his opponents would never be able to look into his eyes and see what he was thinking or what cards he was holding.

The General Lee Steamboat left Saint Louis at four in the afternoon on November 1, 1877. By ten that night, Oliver had won an extensive amount of money and wanted to leave the game and get some rest.

He stood up, gathered up his money and politely told the others at the table, "Gentlemen, it's been fun, but I'm exhausted and will retire for the night. We can resume our game tomorrow if you want a chance to win back your money."

One of the players by the name of Tobias Hamilton, a relatively wealthy, obnoxious man, said, "I'm not ready to call it quits tonight, and neither are you, so sit down and play cards."

Oliver didn't want to make a scene on his first night on the riverboat, but he wouldn't be intimidated by Hamilton. "No, I've already told you that I'm exhausted and ready to rest. I'll take more of your money tomorrow, if you want to continue playing. But right now I'm going to my stateroom, and you best leave me be."

Oliver could tell by the look on Tobias's face that he wasn't used to back-talk. His face turned red and his brow furrowed as he stood to intimidate the young gambler. He was most likely around six foot five and weighed over two hundred and fifty pounds. He had massive hands and arms and was used to getting his way.

One of the other players reached out and pulled on Tobias's arm.

"Sit back down. He said you can take up the game tomorrow. You don't want to cause a scene on the boat and get shot or put to shore."

The man sat down, which was Oliver's cue to leave the poker room.

CHAPTER FOUR

The following day, Oliver returned to the gaming room and bought into a poker game that was short a player. Some small hands produced meager winnings as the game progressed, but it wasn't a good day for the cards to fall. Even though he wanted to stay and play, he wasn't drawing the winning cards for the bigger pots and for some unknown reason he wasn't mentally into playing poker that day either. So he took his money, excused himself from the game and went back to his stateroom for the remainder of the day. Later that night, while he was having his evening meal, Tobias and another man came to his table.

"I've been looking for you," said Tobias in a louder voice than was needed as he stood with his thumbs in his vest pockets. Oliver could tell he fancied himself as someone important by the way he tried to belittle others. But that didn't work on Oliver, especially after the lazy, unaccomplished day he had.

Oliver placed the fork he had in his left hand onto the table neatly beside his plate. "Well, I'm not hard to find. We're on a steamboat, and there are only a few places to go. Now that you have found me, what do you want?"

"I want you in a poker game tonight, and I won't take no for an answer."

Oliver pushed his chair back so he had more room, and pulled his coat back to expose the shoulder gun. "You can demand all you want, but I don't take orders from you. Is that clear?"

"If you think showing me that little pea shooter you have in your shoulder holster gets you off the hook, then you have another thing coming. I don't get scared easily."

"And neither do I," said Oliver. "If you're so adamant about playing me, we'll start at ten tomorrow morning and continue until one of us is broke. I have three thousand dollars with me, so that will be the amount you need to bring to the game."

"That's fine by me." Tobias pointed his finger at Oliver. "I'll see you tomorrow, one way or another." He turned and walked away.

The following morning Oliver was up early and for some reason, he felt lucky. After a hearty breakfast he went to the poker room, where a table had been reserved for him and Tobias. Before heading to the table, Oliver went to the pit boss. "Excuse me, but I want to change the location where me and Tobias will have our game. Would it be all right to move to that one in the corner?"

"Of course. I'll have the dealer move the setup over there."

"I meant that I want a new setup and leave that table as it is."

"Sir, if you suspect cheating, I assure you that we take great pride in running a straight game."

"I know you do, but someone could have tampered with the cards when no one was watching. I want a fair shake at Tobias today."

"I understand, and will have a new setup made ready for you," said the pit boss.

The game got underway, and after two hours, Oliver had begun to win big pots and lose small ones. After another hour of playing, Tobias was down to less than five hundred dollars when Oliver was dealt three tens. The young gambler laid the cards on the table and started tapping with his index finger.

"Stop that tapping. It's annoying," said Tobias.

Oliver smiled and said, "I'll bet two hundred and take two cards." He commenced tapping the table with his index finger again.

Tobias called the bet and said, "I'll take one card."

The dealer passed them the cards, and Oliver never picked his up to see what they were. Instead, he reached out with his left hand, picked up three hundred dollars, and said, "I bet three hundred. I'll take a marker if you don't have that much." He knew that his last remark would make Tobias mad, so he reached into his jacket and made sure his pistol was loose and ready to draw.

Tobias looked at his cards and then pushed in all his money. "I call. I have a king-high flush." He turned his cards over on the table, folded his massive arms across his chest, and leaned back in his chair, smiling from ear to ear so the bystanders could see his good fortune.

Oliver flipped over the three tens with his left hand while his right hand moved closer to his pistol. "I wonder how lucky I was on the draw," he said. He flipped over the first card, which was a five of clubs. He paused briefly and flipped over the next card, a five of spades.

Tobias leaned forward in his chair and slammed his fist on the table, almost turning the table over. "I've had it with you, you no-good cheat!" He abruptly stood up knocking his chair over backward. Tobias moved his hand in one swift motion and went for the gun on his hip. Oliver waited until his hand was on the handle before he pulled his gun and fired into the man's chest.

Tobias stood straight up with his gun hanging uselessly in his hand. He took two steps backward with his eyes about to bug out of their sockets and fell to his knees, then toppled over dead. Oliver opened the cylinder on his gun and ejected the four spent brass hulls. The crowd watching the game gathered around the lifeless body as Oliver gathered his winnings and tucked the money into his jacket pocket.

The steamboat security came running in and detained Oliver while they questioned the guests to find out what had happened. After several hours of intense questions, the riverboat captain confined Oliver to his stateroom, where he was told he would be confined for the rest of the trip. As soon as the boat docked in Memphis, Tennessee, later the next day, he would have to leave and wasn't allowed to get back on.

The following afternoon, three security agents escorted Oliver off the boat as soon as it was secured to the dock and the gangplanks were in place. The docks were littered with stacks of cotton bales as far as he could see in both directions. When he made it to the street, he flagged down a carriage and had it take him to a hotel away from the riverfront area.

Oliver checked into his room and stowed his bag, locking the door on his way out and walking to the street. He needed time to think about what his next move would be. Now he was stranded in a strange town, didn't know one person, and was banned from the steamboat where he had hoped to make a small fortune gambling.

Memphis was alive with music and dives along the street in the center of town. He went into a small place to eat supper, and while there, he overheard two men talking about Little Rock, Arkansas. They discussed how it was growing as a center of commerce because of the reconstruction efforts after the Civil War, even though the war had been over more than ten years. According to them, not only was the city growing in population, but there was a lot of money to make if a man wanted to open saloons that offered gambling, women and whiskey.

Oliver returned to his room and sat on the bed for a long time, trying to figure out where to go and what he would do once he was there. Little Rock might be his next adventure.

The following morning, he walked along the docks and then circled back toward the hotel, where he found a café to eat breakfast. After breakfast, he approached a small group of elderly Black men sitting in a small park whittling on pieces of cedar. "Excuse me, could I get some information from you fellers?" he asked.

One of the men pointed to a bench. "Have a seat and ask what you want."

Oliver decided to be honest with the men. "I'm a gambler and got kicked off the *General Lee* yesterday after I killed a man who drew his gun on me. I'm curious if you know anything about Little Rock, Arkansas."

"What do you want to know? We don't know much, but some of us have been there."

"For starters, how do I get there, and do they allow gambling?"

One of the men pointed toward a railroad bridge that spanned the river. "The quickest and easiest way is to use the CRI&P Railroad. My sister lives there, and it takes me about eight hours or so to get there on the train. As for gambling, the city is wide open for mischief, and you won't have trouble finding a game. One piece of advice I've got for you is to go ahead and cross the river when you get there. The folks on the east side are poor farmers and don't have much."

"Much obliged for the information." Oliver got up.

"Young feller," said one of the other men. "I notice you ain't wearing a gun, and I wouldn't go there dressed like you is. Wearing a suit is a dead giveaway that you ain't from these parts of the country and especially the south. I advise you to buy some new clothes that will help you blend in, and you'll definitely need a hip gun in Little Rock if you plan on gambling there."

Oliver nodded his head. "Could you direct me to a clothing store and a gun shop?" asked Oliver.

"Go down that street right over there," said one of the men, pointing to the east. "The place is called Mrs. Sallie's, and you tell her Herman sent you. She'll have everything you need."

"Thanks, I'll go there now."

Oliver went shopping at Mrs. Sallie's, buying himself some riding clothes, a gun, and a holster that he could wear on his hip. After that, he returned to his hotel room and practiced drawing the new pistol. Now equipped with a gun on his hip and the shoulder gun, he figured he was ready for anything at the poker tables.

The following day, he started to hit the dives in Memphis looking for poker games. The gambler spent the next five weeks in Memphis until his luck began to fade. When it finally ran out, he went to the train station, where he purchased a train ticket to Little Rock, Arkansas.

CHAPTER FIVE

Oliver spent sixteen months in Little Rock enjoying the different saloons and gambling halls scattered throughout the city. But controversy finally came his way one night when he had to shoot his way out of a high-stakes poker game. When the smoke cleared, two men had been shot, and one was dead.

The local marshal questioned the patrons who witnessed the shooting while Oliver spent the night in jail.

When he was released around noon the following day, he went to the house where he had been staying with a woman that worked at one of the saloons he played at. Her name was Missy Joe, and she was originally from Southern Arkansas. He and Missy had a good relationship but were not in love. He paid her for room and board while enjoying her companionship.

Two nights after the shooting when Missy had gotten off work, she and Oliver walked together to their home. Two men were waiting in the shadows for Oliver.

As Oliver and Missy started to climb the steps that led to the front door, the men came out of the shadows and started firing their guns. Oliver pulled his weapon and returned fire, aiming at the muzzle flashes of the guns of the two assailants.

The shooting stopped, and as the smoke cleared, Oliver saw Missy lying in the yard with blood on her chest. He went to her and fell to his knees to see if she was alive. Two bullets had hit her in the chest, ending her young life.

The gambler lifted her up and placed her lifeless body on his legs as he sobbed and held her close. It was all his fault. He had made enemies, and they had come for him, although he didn't know who the shooters were yet. All he knew was that his girlfriend was dead, and the two men who attacked them were also lying in the yard.

Neighbors by the names of John and Becky came into the yard. John had brought a lantern with him. Becky started to cry when she saw Missy dead. John put his arm around his wife to console her.

"Becky, go in the house and get a quilt so we can cover Missy up," said John. Then he went to Oliver. "You have to let her go. There ain't nothing you can do for her now. Come with me, and let's see if we know who the shooters are."

Oliver leaned over and kissed Missy on the lips and got up. Becky exited the house and laid the quilt over the dead woman's corpse.

John and Oliver went to the two dead men and turned them so they could see their faces.

Oliver said, "I don't recognize either of these men. Do you know who they are?

"No, I've never seen them before. Maybe the law will know who they are when they get here. I sent my boy after them when the shooting started," said John.

Oliver pulled out his pistol and reloaded the spent

shells. More neighbors were in the yard when three lawmen arrived.

Oliver watched as John stood holding the lantern while the lawmen went through the dead men's pockets. When they finished, one of them came to Oliver.

"I'm mighty sorry about Miss Missy getting killed. Those two are the Ham brothers. They are the brothers of the man you killed in that shoot-out in the saloon a few days ago. It just so happened that these two were in jail the night you killed their brother."

"That explains everything. Thanks for coming and investigating this."

"We're just doing our job. The undertaker will be here soon to collect the bodies," said the deputy.

"Thanks again. If it's all right with you all, I'll get my things from the house and check into a hotel for the night," said Oliver.

"That's fine by us. You can probably check with Samuel Hutchings, the undertaker, tomorrow and settle up with the burial arrangements," said the deputy.

Oliver checked into the hotel, but sleep didn't come until almost daylight. After he had breakfast, he walked to the mortician's parlor.

"Good morning, sir. What can I do for you?"

"I'm here to pay you to bury Missy. How much do I owe you, and when can you complete the burial?" asked Oliver.

"I have her all cleaned up and in a nice coffin. Everyone loved that girl, and if you want, I can bury her at one o'clock this afternoon."

"That will be fine. How much do I owe you?" asked Oliver.

"That will be seventeen dollars, including my special carriage to transport the body to the graveyard," said Samuel.

Oliver paid the man. "I'll see you at the graveyard at one.

"Yes, sir."

Oliver walked back to the hotel and lay down; he needed to think about what to do. Little Rock was not going to be good for him in the future. He would attend the funeral and then leave town.

When the brief service was over, Oliver went back to the hotel. He sat on the bed and wept before gathering his things and leaving town on a horse he had purchased six months ago to get around town.

CHAPTER SIX

For gamblers like Oliver Golden, there came a time to know when to fold and leave for greener pastures, and that time had come for him. His girlfriend was dead and he had nothing to keep him at Little Rock any longer. Hot Springs was the talk of Little Rock, and by all accounts, the money flowed at the poker tables like the hot spring water flowed from the ground.

Not being used to horse travel and sleeping in the wild, the first few days on the road almost made him turn back. He was sore, and the hard ground to sleep on was nothing compared to the nice beds that he was accomplished to in the hotel. It took him considerable time to find rest from each day's journey with his meager bedding.

Oliver had been fortunate to put together over ten thousand dollars in winnings since he'd left Saint Louis, but within the first month he was in Hot Springs, he learned that the town's gaming business wasn't friendly to outside card sharks. All the big gaming houses required a percentage of the winnings, and if a player didn't pay up, they would feel the wrath of the goons who worked for the crime lords. The first time Oliver refused to pay, three men beat him unconscious and took over two thousand dollars from him.

He was laid up for over two weeks as he healed from the beating but used that time to watch the street from his room at the Arlington Hotel. He would also go to one of the springs each day and soak in the hot water and listen to conversations. The water soothed his aching body from the beating. Oliver waited for three weeks after the debacle of the beating and robbery before putting a plan in place to get his money back.

He spent a lot of time talking to travelers passing through Hot Springs and finally decided how he would execute his departure. And once he left, he would go to Texarkana, Texas, and then northwest from there. Rumors about silver and gold in south-central Colorado seemed to dominate the conversations he'd been overhearing.

Lessons learned on his journey from Little Rock to Hot Springs were that he needed a better bed roll, shelter from the rain, more cooking utensils, and an adequate supply of provisions to eat along the way. That meant he would need to buy a packhorse to carry everything he required for his journey.

It took him two days to acquire the essential items for his trip. Then it was a matter of getting the money back that the men who worked for the local kingpin had stolen from him. After careful observation, he determined that Frank "The Boss" Flynn was the big boss behind all the organized crime and gaming in Hot Springs. He owned his own saloon, called the Palace, and that was where Oliver would retrieve his money.

It took him another week before the right time came along to make his play. As the weekend started on Friday night, many big-time gamblers arrived in town to soak in the hot, soothing mineral water and play cards. Oliver saw this as his opportunity to get his money back and had both horses loaded and ready to leave town as soon as possible. Since Hot Springs was located in a heavily wooded area surrounded by mountains and boulders, he easily found a good place to hide his horses until he was prepared to depart.

He sat to the east of the Palace Saloon among the rocks and watched who came and went from the place.

At dusk the two men who had beat him up left through the back door of the Palace. They were carrying big canvas satchels, and began to make their rounds collecting payoff money from the saloons and gaming establishments. Oliver followed them but stayed in the shadows as much as possible or sometimes he would have to hide in an alley so he could watch them. The two men had already visited seven establishments when they turned down an alley and Oliver saw his chance. He ran to the end of the opposite block and entered the alley from the opposite direction to advance on the men.

He had his gun in his hand, hidden behind his back. When he was within fifteen feet of the two thugs, one of them pointed his finger at Oliver.

"Stand to the side. We're coming through."

Oliver moved to the side, and as the two men walked past, he swung the gun and hit the man closest to him in the back of his head. The other man turned with a billy club in his hand and was struck across the face with the gun. He tried to fight back but was no match for Oliver, who hit him multiple times with his weapon.

A quick inspection of the satchels was all he needed to see that they were both full of money, and it was time to say goodbye to Hot Springs, Arkansas.

He ran where he had left his horses and hid the satchels among his provisions on the back of the packhorse. If someone saw him leave the city, they would think he was just another weary soul leaving town broke and in despair. He walked the horses west until they were clear of the towns boundary's and then picked up the pace to get as far away as possible before dawn. The Ouachita Mountains would be his principal difficulty, but while he was recuperating he'd asked the locals and found out the best course to travel.

He rode southwest toward Arkadelphia, Arkansas, which lay nestled in the foothills of the Ouachita. It took him four days to journey through the mountains to his destination. The terrain was an obstacle at first, but as he got closer to the little town the path got easier to traverse. Whenever he encountered another traveler, he would ask for directions.

Oliver only stayed one night in Arkadelphia, restocking his provisions at a small general store before heading for Prescott, Arkansas. It took him two days to travel the thirty-one miles.

Travel by horseback was beginning to get much easier for him and provided him ample time to think about his future. He wasn't sure anymore if gambling was going to be the profession that would get him to a ripe old age. He thought about the two satchels he'd taken off the goons in Hot Springs. More than forty-two hundred dollars was stashed in the bags, but he knew that money came at a hefty price if the Flynn gang caught up with him.

It seemed that everywhere he went, there was violence, and a man living at the poker table should expect controversy and danger. He needed to start being more aware of his surroundings and stay out of trouble. The violence associated with being a gambler had already taken someone's life that he cared for.

Prescott was only a stopping place to buy a few provisions and get a good night's sleep at the only hotel in the little town. He stayed away from the saloon and only went to one store to buy what he needed. The fewer people who saw him, the better off he was in case someone came inquiring about him.

The railroad coming through was the reason for building Prescott, and even now, some businesses operate in tents. Oliver ate breakfast in one of the three cafés that served food in a tent with crude wooden tables. After a good meal of eggs and ham, he headed to Texarkana.

CHAPTER SEVEN

Texarkana proved to be a helpful stop in his quest to make money. He was hired at one of the local establishments to run the gaming tables and given twenty percent of everything the house brought in from the games of chance.

Oliver had been in Texarkana five months playing the different saloons and gaming houses before he was offered the job as gaming boss at the Ace High Saloon. Over his first six months as the gaming manager, Oliver established himself as a serious businessman and didn't play any poker. He trained dealers, watched for cheats and made sure the waitresses kept the players in liquor.

Two men came into the tavern area one night while he was standing at the counter talking to the bartender, George. They stood at the polished countertop, placed one dirty boot on the footrest and ordered a whiskey. When their drinks were delivered, one of the men said, "We're looking for a friend who likes to play poker. His name is Oliver Golden. Have you seen him around at any of the tables?"

George wiped off a drop of spilled whiskey where he stood. "I ain't never seen Oliver Golden play cards here."

"Is that a fact? I take it you know who he is?"

"Yep, I know who he is, but he doesn't play cards at our tables."

Oliver could hear the men talking to George but kept his back to the men so they couldn't see his face. He watched out of the corner of his eye as the bartender continued to wipe off the top of the counter, never once looking his way. What was he up to, and why had he told the men that Oliver didn't play cards there? In all honesty, he didn't play cards. It was his job to act as the floor boss and oversee the gaming. These men were trouble, and he could tell George was trying to get them to leave in a friendly way.

Both men downed their drinks and dropped money into the empty glasses. They made their way around the room, looking at everyone playing the different games. Oliver went to the back room and watched from behind a curtain. The bartender brought two empty bottles into the room and placed them in a crate.

"Those two men are looking for you, and if I'm as good as I think I am, they're bounty hunters wanting your hide."

"Yeah, I heard them ask about me. But I'm not wanted by any law I know of, so I wonder who they work for."

"You may want to make yourself scarce for a while. If they go to the other saloons and gin mills asking questions, they're liable to find out you run the gaming here and come back for you mighty quick."

"I'd like to know who sent them after me, but that may be hard to find out unless I confront them."

"All I can say about that is don't do it here. The boss doesn't want any gunplay inside. That runs away business."

"I understand. I'll think of a plan to keep those two out of here," said Oliver.

The bartender returned to work cleaning and filling glasses while Oliver stayed in the back room.

Crap, here I go again, he thought. *Putting it off is useless, so I'll wait until the two men return this way.*

He pulled his gun and checked that it was fully loaded, then went outside, standing on the boardwalk to wait until the two men returned to look for him. It was a short wait. Ten minutes later, they came out of a saloon about a half block away. Oliver headed toward them with the shoulder gun in his hand, hidden behind his back.

"I'm Oliver Golden. I hear that you fellers have been going around town inquiring about me?"

"That's right, we have," said one of the men as they took one step apart.

"Who are you working for, and why are you looking for me?" asked Oliver.

"We were hired by Tobias Hamilton's brother to kill you."

Oliver started to laugh. "I hope he paid you in advance since you'll never be able to enjoy your blood money," he said as he came around with his pistol and fired point-blank into the face of the man doing the talking. He quickly pointed the still-smoking gun barrel at the other man, who had pulled his gun — but not fast enough. Two bullets entered the bounty hunter's chest. Oliver didn't wait around to see if they were dead. Instead, he holstered his weapon and returned to the saloon to gather his things. It was time to leave and find another town to call home.

He hurried to his room upstairs in the saloon, packed his bag, and brought it into the gaming room to collect his pay. Next, he sent one of the boys who cleaned inside the saloon to the livery stable to tell the hustler to get his horses ready for travel.

When he went back outside, he saw the city marshal standing by the bodies and walked up to him.

"Hello, Marshal. Those two men were hired to kill me and came here looking for me. You can ask the bartender, and he'll tell you the truth about them asking questions about me. I met them on the boardwalk; you can imagine the rest of the story. I shot both of them in self-defense, and if it's okay with you, I'll go ahead and leave town."

"I don't like gunplay in my town even if it was self-defense. You're free to go, and I suggest you don't come back," said the marshal in a stern voice.

Oliver nodded and walked toward the livery stable. As he passed by the mercantile, he stuck his head in the doorway. "Would you put me some provisions together while I go after my horse? I need enough food for a week."

With both horses in tow, he stopped long enough to load his supplies and then headed west out of town. That night while he relaxed in his camp, he reflected on his life and what he had to do to get past all the gunplay. He knew that he was a little quick to take matters into his own hands, and a gambler was always fair game to someone who had lost their life savings.

He traveled from town to town for six weeks until he stopped in Albany, Texas. He had only been there five days when he killed Jeff Gaines and had to hit the road again.

CHAPTER EIGHT

Oliver tossed and turned in bed the night after he killed Jeff. The dreams kept clouding his sleep and kept occupying his unconscious state to the point that he couldn't rest. They were the same dreams he had experienced the first time he killed someone and had to run to get away from the mob. In the early morning hours, covered in sweat and breathing hard, he came awake and lay in the confines of his room, staring up at the dark ceiling.

Paul Gaines's ranch hands had ridden north last night, and he presumed they stayed on the trail or maybe spent the night in another town. He never heard them return to Albany, which was good. If they were north, maybe he would ride west from Albany toward the Gaines Ranch. They would never think he would ride in that direction in a hundred years.

Oliver looked at his pocket watch to see it was already five in the morning. It would be daylight by the time he gathered his things and saddled his horse. The safest thing to do was leave town by riding east, then circle around to the south and west. Hopefully there would be someplace within a three days' ride where he could buy supplies.

With the sun coming up big and bright, he skirted Albany to the east until he couldn't see any of the town's buildings. He turned to the south and then turned west where he found the west road of the city. It was well-traveled by the look of the wagon ruts and horse tracks, and he took his time and let his horse lope until he reached a fork in the road. Oliver studied a sign on the side of the road, with the arrow pointing toward the ranch painted in red. The ranch brand was burned into the wood, *Gaines Ranch*, with its *Rocking G* symbol seared into the wood by a running iron

It was decision time. Did the hunted man turn north and get closer to the ranch headquarters, or did he ride farther west and come in from the back side?

No one should know what he looked like — at least he hoped that would be the case if he saw some cowhands on the range. The only two who had seen him were unlikely to ever see him again. He urged his horse to go north, and after a mile, he turned west into the scattered mesquites, cedars, and hackberry trees that grew on the range where the cattle were grazing.

The land was mostly rolling hills, with a few gullies from runoff water and an occasional small mesa. When he had ridden to the top of one of the hills, he stopped his horse and looked over the expanse of land to see cattle grazing everywhere he looked. There must have been thousands of head of cattle on the range, and he was in awe of the sight before him.

He didn't want to ride through the middle of the herd for fear of spooking them into running. So he rode west, keeping away from the bawling bovine. Oliver had never been around this many cattle in his life. In fact, eating a steak was as close as he had ever been to a cow. Some of these cows had massive horns that protruded three feet in both directions. Some others had no horns, markedly different from the long-horned cattle.

The grass they grazed on rose almost as high as their bellies, and he had no idea what kind it was. Once clear of where the cattle grazed and staying partially hidden by the rolling hills, Oliver continued west until he could turn north enough to return to the same trajectory as before he rode up on the cattle.

His horse picked up the pace, and he rode into a valley that happened to have a creek with water in it. He let the horse have his fill before he crossed over the creek and rode up a grassy hill covered in mesquite trees. It was good that the mesquites weren't thick, or he would have gotten stuck with thorns.

Just as they climbed to the crest of a hill, Oliver stopped the horse because off in the distance, he could make out buildings scattered over a couple of acres. They must have served as the Gaines Ranch headquarters. Now he knew why the man in town had called it a hacienda. From his vantage spot, the main house was sprawling, built in the Spanish architectural style.

Oliver eased his horse back off the hill and tied him to a limb, and climbed back up the hillside to watch the ranch compound. He could make out shapes of men in the yard and at the corral, but he was so far away that it was hard to see what they were doing.

Oliver walked back to his horse and thought about his next move. What if he rode up the creek bed and got closer to the buildings? If he stayed in the creek bottom, he might get close enough to see and still be out of sight of anyone in the yard. He wanted to gain as much knowledge as possible about the man who wanted him dead. The more he knew about Paul Gaines and his hired men, the better. This was taking a big chance by getting close to the house, but he was a gambler after all.

He went back to his horse, mounted up, and walked him in the water, leaning over the saddle as far as possible in hopes that no one would see him. When he had traveled a hundred and fifty yards, the creek changed directions and the terrain was changing also. It was time to stop and look at the ranch yard and buildings.

There was a large Spanish-style house, three large barns, and two other structures he assumed were bunkhouses where the men lived. Another building had smoke coming from a chimney and from a stovepipe. This building had to be a cook shack and mess hall where the men ate their meals. Oliver was hungry for a meal himself, and after thirty minutes of watching the ranch headquarters, he returned to his horse, headed back to where he'd entered the water, and rode south away from the Gaines Ranch.

CHAPTER NINE

Oliver rode southwest when he was out of sight of the ranch buildings. He kept riding, seeing herds of cattle scattered throughout the rolling hills. Was it possible that all these cows were part of the Gaines Ranch?

The creek he'd seen earlier by the ranch house had also changed its course, and now he could see it to his right. He had stayed within eye sight of it since leaving the ranch yard and used it as a reference point. This would be an excellent time to fill his canteen and water his horse before he went farther southwest.

He had to ride up and over a few brush-covered hills to get to the narrow valley where the stream of water was.

The creek was much wider at this location than it had been when he was closer to the hacienda. Which was odd, since it was only about twelve feet wide at the ranch headquarters. After Oliver and his horse took on water, he mounted and rode along the stream out of curiosity, wondering why it was broader. Close to two miles downstream, he rode upon an earthen dam that had been erected across the channel to back up the flow of the creek. What a neat idea, to build a reservoir out on the range so the livestock would have abundant water.

It was constructed with a wooden spillway, allowing water to overflow, and the small creek still ran wet to irrigate the land west of here.

"You on the horse, keep your hands where we can see them," came a voice behind Oliver.

He didn't move in his saddle or turn his head to see who was behind him. Instead he said, "I'm not here for trouble. I was just passing through and admiring the handywork of your dam."

"What's your name, and where're you headed?" asked another voice.

For some reason, Oliver decided to use his middle name. "I'm Canyon, and I'm heading to Colorado."

"Well, our boss doesn't like drifters riding across his range, so I suggest you get going and don't look back for the next eight miles until you get off the Gaines Ranch."

"Not a problem. I'll be on my way." Oliver touched the sides of his horse with his heels, and it had taken a couple of steps when he heard one of the men say, "Hold up, we have two guns on you. Turn that horse around so we can see your face."

Oliver thought he had heard that voice before, and as he pulled the bridle reins to the left, he reached into his jacket, removed the shoulder gun, and cocked the hammer back. The horse turned, and Oliver recognized the two men. They had been with Jeff Gaines in the saloon the day he'd killed Jeff.

It took the men a few seconds to recognize Oliver, but that delay cost them their lives. Oliver brought up his gun and fired at the first man, and as he toppled out of the saddle, Oliver fired and missed the second man. He fired again at the same time the cowboy fired at him.

Oliver felt the impact of the slug as it pushed him off balance in the saddle. The burning sensation and pain almost caused him to lose consciousness, but he managed to stay awake and make sure that both men were dead.

He looked down at his shirt to see blood covering the left side of his abdomen and knew he had to get away from the two dead cowboys in case someone had heard the shots. He kept his hand on his side where the bullet had entered, but it didn't stop the bleeding.

It was hard to ride the horse and hold pressure on the wound. Dizziness and anxiety caused him to think about death on the open range by himself. He thought about what his mama told him about the man in black who visited her before she died. That brought back memories, but more importantly — who was the man in black? Was he from God or from Satan?

Stop it, he told himself. He needed to find a place to hold up and see how badly he'd been hit.

He stopped long enough to retrieve the fancy-dress linen shirt from his bag and tore the material into strips. As fast as he could, he unbuttoned the shirt he had on and removed it. He held a bandage made from the material of his shirt to the bullet wound until he could get the linen strips tied so that the dressing was tight against the wound. While he was applying the dressing, he felt a little farther around his side, and sure enough, there was also an exit wound that was also bleeding. He pushed some of the material into both holes and then wrapped strips of shirt around his torso to slow the bleeding down so he could continue to look for a place to hold up.

Off to the west, there appeared to be an outcropping of rocks or a small mesa, which might provide an excellent place to camp so he could tend to his wound.

It took him almost an hour to get there, since he had to go slow and try not to fall off his horse. As he got closer, the mound of dirt and stone got larger but something seemed to be out of place. He turned to look in the direction he'd come from and then at the mesa before him. He had ridden to the south of the plateau and didn't notice doing it. He must have blacked out for a time, and his horse had gone where it wanted to.

Oliver touched his heels to the horse and continued to ride around the large mound of soil and rocks that formed the mesa. His horse moved forward to an opening in the side of the plateau, and Oliver let him pick his path through the rocky soil. It was a tight squeeze, but the mesa opened up into a trail that led somewhere that his horse wanted to go. His legs scraped along the edges of the chasm since the path was narrow. The vast mounds were only about twenty feet tall with an outcropping of rock; the rest of the area was littered with grass and brush. Thirty yards in, the narrow pathway opened into a minor basin that was a fourth of an acre in size. The clearing's floor was covered with lush green grass except for two willow trees near a patch of ground where water seeped from the earth and ran off in a natural ditch. His horse went to the water and began to drink. Oliver tried to dismount but fell from the saddle onto the soft ground.

Getting to his feet was going to take a lot of his strength, but it was still much better than trying to crawl on his hands and knees. He sat on the ground for a few minutes, looking around the small clearing. Most likely no one knew about this place, and it would be an excellent location to hole up for a few days if he could find shelter.

Oliver grabbed the stirrup and pulled himself to a standing position while still holding on to the horse's reins. A shadow caught his eye at the far end of the opening, which was only about sixty feet away. He led his horse in that direction but had to stop twice before he got there. It was a rock ledge, bare of grass, with an overhang of stone that could provide him shelter in case it rained. He tied his horse so he could investigate further. His side was hurting so badly that he thought he would pass out. Oliver put his arm around his horse's neck so he wouldn't fall.

"It looks like this will be our new home for a while, boy. I'll try to get the saddle off you as soon as I can."

After an hour of alternately working and resting, Oliver finally had the saddle and the rest of his things under the ledge. All he had to do now was gather enough wood to build a fire.

CHAPTER TEN

Oliver sat on the rock slab's surface, trying to rest enough to finish preparing his camp. When he'd done all he could, the only thing he lacked was brush to place across the narrow entrance so his horse couldn't leave.

The pain and discomfort in his side seemed to be getting worse. He rose to his feet on weak legs and made his way to the path that had led him into the clearing earlier. He scattered dead brush in front of the trail, and that would have to work for now. Oliver returned to his fire on the ledge and placed his coffeepot filled with water to get hot beside the fire.

Before sitting down, he removed his shirt and the bandage he had applied to the wound earlier in the day. The dressing was covered in both dried and fresh blood.

Once seated, he took salt from his food bag and put a pinch of it in the hot water. After tearing a fresh piece of cloth from his linen shirt, he soaked the rag in the salt water and washed his wound with it. The sting from the salt caused him to grit his teeth and it irritated the wound, but he knew he had to clean the affected skin and bullet hole.

The wound was clean, but blood was still seeping from the hole left by the bullet. The skin around the hole was red and inflamed. Oliver sat with the rag pressed against his injured side. He thought about searing the wound, but with what? Then he remembered the pocketknife he had purchased in Little Rock, which should be in his travel bag. Sure enough, the folding knife was in the bag, and after putting the blade in the fire until it glowed red, he applied to the injury, and the searing pain made him pass out.

Oliver woke up as the sun was beginning to set in the west. After examining the wound again, he saw the bleeding had stopped, but the area was still red and inflamed, most likely from the knife blade he had used earlier. Moving the pot closer to the coals, he reheated the water and felt around the hole where the bullet had exited his side. That wound wasn't bleeding, so he would bandage it after he had washed the entrance and exit wounds.

Once his wounds were clean and covered in fresh bandages, he ate a can of beans for supper and prepared his bed. Next, he made sure to place a full canteen next to his bedroll and put more wood on the fire.

Oliver awoke during the night covered in sweat and shaking like he was freezing. Drinking some water from his canteen helped cool off the heat inside his mouth. It wasn't long until the fever had taken over his body and mind and gave him visions of death while sitting at a card table. He would wake up, go back to sleep, and dream about death. In the dream, he was fighting for his last breath and seeing his last tomorrow. Tossing and turning, he kept seeing his afterlife as he stood on the mountain looking over the Jordan River into heaven. He reached out his hand to an angelic figure dressed in white, but it vanished.

Oliver's eyes opened, and he sat up. The sun beamed down on him. His clothes were sweaty, and his mouth was parched from thirst. After taking large gulps of water, he lay back down but stayed awake. What could the visions have meant? Was the figure dressed in white an angel, or was it God Almighty? He had questions, but no one was there to give him answers. The fever had subsided, and he lay on his damp bed wondering what he needed to do to change what he saw in his vision. With that thought, he closed his eyes and went back to sleep.

Oliver woke again, and it was dark when he opened his eyes this time. The campfire had gone out and had to be started again before he could make coffee and eat something. He assumed he had only slept through one day, but it could have been multiple days by the empty feeling of his stomach.

The flames from the fire gave him enough light to go to the spring and fill the coffeepot and his canteen. He needed to eat, but only had a can of beans and jerky left. That would do for tonight, but tomorrow he would have to try to kill an animal for food. He wasn't sure he'd be strong enough to do it.

The beans and coffee took care of his hunger, and he was tired, so he lay back down and went to sleep.

The following morning his encampment was shrouded in fog, and it took him a little while to get his fire going with the damp wood. Coffee and jerky for breakfast were of little help to squelch his hunger, but it did give him some nutrition. After eating, he emptied his coffeepot and once again heated salt water to clean his injury. His wound looked better today, and he could clean it well without passing out.

Later in the day, once he put on clean bandages, he went to the trail that came into his box canyon and adjusted the brush so that small animals could come in for water.

CHAPTER ELEVEN

Oliver had a fever off and on for the rest of the day, but he managed to stay awake and watch for animals to come into the encampment for water. Late in the afternoon, he filled his coffeepot with water and dropped pieces of jerky into the pot. There were a few wild onions growing along the tiny stream from the spring that he also put in the pot with the jerky.

He figured if he boiled the stringy beef strips along with the onions, he could drink the liquid, and it would fill his stomach enough to reduce his hunger pangs.

Not wanting to waste his coffee, the jerky and onion liquid was all he drank that night. It was filling, and he had let his fire burn down to coals when he heard the faint sound of something walking through the narrow trail that led to his camp.

Oliver pulled his gun and stuck it under his blanket so he could cock the hammer quietly. With the weapon ready to fire he remained still until he could see whatever it was that was coming for water. The wait was a short one—within a minute, three deer came walking into the clearing and stopped when they smelled the smoke from the fire. Oliver sat still, hoping they'd come closer, but the deer were hesitant and turned to leave. He held his breath and stayed still, and in a few minutes they returned and stopped and looked right at him before they walked to the spring.

Oliver waited until he had a perfect shot. The little doe turned sideways, and he aimed at the deer's heart and pulled the trigger. The deer went down on its front legs, and he fired a second shot, hitting the animal in the side of its head. The remaining two deer ran toward the trail and were gone.

Taking his folding knife, Oliver began to skin his food for the next few days. As weak as he was, it took him over two hours to skin the deer and bring the meat close to his fire. He realized the meat would spoil if he didn't do something with it, so he began to cook it in his small skillet.

The flour sack he had brought his supplies in would have to be used to store the prepared meat. Sometime after midnight, he had fried all the meat and even filled his stomach before he lay down exhausted.

The following morning, he used the last of his salt in hot water to clean his wounds. The affected area was not as inflamed, and there were signs of scabs forming over the holes. He also used the last of his clean bandages. When he had the wounds taken care of, he put the soiled bandages in what was left of the hot salt water, hoping it would clean and sterilize the cloth.

When he looked up, the sun was directly overhead, and he left his vest and shirt off as he ate deer meat and drank from his canteen. The combination of getting shot and not having adequate food and medicine had taken much of his strength away. He figured he had hidden for four days, but it could have been more. After eating, he strapped the holster on his hip and checked that the gun was fully loaded. It was time to get some exercise and start rebuilding his strength, meaning he would have to walk in circles inside his encampment.

After twenty minutes of walking, he had to sit down. Getting shot had taken more out of him than he first thought. Sitting on his bedroll, leaning against his saddle eating deer meat, he dozed off to sleep and the dream he had two nights before returned to him.

Abruptly his eyes opened and he was covered in sweat. Was God Almighty telling him something in his dream? Was God telling him to change his ways and become a different person? He pondered on those two questions as he sat there and wiped the sweat from his face. Oliver had never been a man of faith or attended many church services, but he had read the Bible extensively growing up. His ma had made him read it as part of his education since it was the only book his family owned. It was strange that the dream had been about death and seeing the Lord in his glory, but after all it was just a dream. Being consumed with fever wouldn't change his thoughts about religion. Eventually he closed his eyes and fell off to sleep.

The next three days were spent walking and resting. There was still plenty of deer meat, but after four days, Oliver began worrying about how long it would stay good, even though it was cooked.

With the bandage removed from his wounds so they could get open air and scab over faster, he removed his clothes and took them to the small stream. He took his time, washed the soiled clothing, and placed it on some bushes to dry.

It had been over a week since he'd been shot, and his

strength was gradually returning to him. He removed the brush that he had put up to block the trail so he could leave his hiding place. The passage along the narrow path opened to the vast range of grass, mesquite, cedars, and hackberries. It was a good guess that men from the Gaines' ranch were still hunting for him, and he didn't want to be seen outside of the encampment. That was enough reason to stay hidden in the box canyon for a few more days until he regained more strength. There was no way he wanted to tackle unfriendly riders in the shape he was in just yet.

The deer meat lasted two more days before it began to smell and turn color. At that point, Oliver decided it was time to investigate outside his box canyon and see if he could shoot something else to eat. He left his hiding place and sat close to the trail entrance, watching the range for movement. A covey of quail took flight to his left, alarming him. That might have meant danger, so he hurried back to the narrow trail that led to his hiding place. He grabbed a handful of sage grass and swept the trail floor as he backed along the path, erasing his boot prints. A few minutes later, he heard a voice and then another. With gun in hand and the hammer cocked, he waited.

"I don't see anything that looks like that feller might have come this way. I say we head on west and then circle to the north before we head back to camp."

"Yeah, I agree. Who knows where that fast gun went or who he is. The boss thinks it was someone casing out the herd so they could steal a few."

Oliver couldn't make out the rest of their conversation as they began riding away from his hiding place. He gave them a few minutes more and then went back to the mouth of the path with his gun ready to fire. No one was in sight, so he skirted the plateau until he saw the men off in the distance.

That was a close call, and he knew he would have to be careful about shooting something to eat. He had heard them say they had a camp. Did that mean back at the ranch headquarters, or did they have a base camp on the range somewhere?

Oliver walked along the plateau, looking for a way to climb higher so he could see farther away. Unfortunately, it was too steep for him, since any rigorous movement could reopen his wounds.

He turned and walked in the opposite direction until he arrived where the plateau sloped out to lower ground. With his hand to his forehead to shield his eyes, he looked west and scanned back toward the east, where something caught his attention. He could just barely make out two men on horseback.

That was most likely the two men he had heard, but he wasn't sure, so he stayed where he was until they were out of sight. If there were more riders out on the range, he should be able to see them. He waited until dusk and then had started back to his camp when he saw a rabbit eating some fresh grass under a clump of brush. One shot, and he had dinner. When he gathered the hare from the ground, another rabbit ran off, and he fired at it. Now he had food for today and tomorrow. It was time to return to his camp and clean the animals, but first he had to wipe away all his tracks. Those two shots might draw someone's attention, and he couldn't afford to have someone coming to investigate.

He piled brush about midway down the narrow path that led to his camp. If someone did try to get to him, he would hear them coming as they stepped on the dry leaves and branches.

That night with both rabbits cooked and his belly full,

he lay on his bed and looked up at the sky. It was a beautiful sight to gaze at the stars and enjoy the things God had made. He paused. That was something he had never thought about before. Had the dream really changed how he was seeing things?

CHAPTER TWELVE

F ive more days passed without incident, and he didn't see any more riders. Oliver killed another small deer and had a sufficient amount of food. It had been almost three weeks since he'd been wounded, and he was healing better than he had figured. The weather was hot and humid, and there was no breeze in the box canyon so the heat was brutal. Each day, he would go out and watch the range for riders. On this day, he climbed up the side of the mesa and found an animal trail. The good thing was the plateau wasn't but about twenty feet tall. He sat on the lush grass and looked at the landscape in all directions. To the south, he could make out what looked like a creek or gully that continued out of sight.

When he had watched enough and the sun was making him unbearably hot, he began to start down. That's when he spotted two men on horses coming his way. They didn't seem to be in a hurry or have any destination in mind since they weren't following a trail or any given path. They were just riding and talking. Oliver lay on his stomach so they wouldn't see him hiding atop the mesa. When they turned their horses toward the entrance of the boxed canyon, Oliver used that opportunity to go farther in toward his camp and out of their sight. Now if they looked up, he wouldn't be seen.

"I hear that the boss has assigned Weasel and Chandler the task of finding the gambler who killed Jeff," said one of the men.

Oliver stayed still, and the riders must have stopped because he could no longer hear horse hooves in the dirt. Oliver eased closer to the edge of the mesa and saw them taking swigs of water from their canteens.

"Yep, and that's not all. Weasel left three days ago for town with the orders to not return until that man was dead. The boss also sent Chandler to look around the area where those two idiots who ran with Jeff got killed."

"So Chandler is out here?"

"Yep, he's around here somewhere, and if I'm correct, he's most likely holed up with a good advantage point where he can use his looking glass watching for anyone who crosses the range."

"He better not get any ideas if he sees us. That man is about half nuts."

"I would rather have him after me than Weasel. He's downright mean, and you better watch your back with him and that knife he carries. I hear he's fast with a gun but deadly with that knife."

"We better get going so we can return to the dam by dark. I'm hungry and don't want to miss supper."

Oliver watched them ride off while he thought about what he had learned. If this Chandler feller was out on the range trying to find him, he would have to stop leaving his hiding place until he was ready to depart for good. Oliver stayed where he was and decided that when he did go, he would ride southwest and intersect with the creek he had seen. It was almost dark when he finally came off the mesa and returned to the box canyon.

The third evening after he had heard the riders talking, Oliver packed up what deer meat he had left and the rest of his supplies and saddled his horse. This time he led him through the narrow passage before he got into the saddle. It had been almost four weeks since he got shot, and most of the soreness was gone. Oliver felt good again and had spent a lot of time thinking about going on to Colorado and working the silver and gold mines. Being laid up in hiding had also given him time to practice drawing the gun on his hip as well as the gun in his shoulder holster.

As the sky turned dark, he left, hoping no one would see him ride away from the mesa. He had a good map of the creek bed stuck in his mind from watching it over the past few days, and it would be easy to find at night. Unfortunately, the moon hadn't come up yet, and it was pitch dark. He let his horse find its way through the mesquite trees.

Sure enough, he found the creek bed, consisting mostly of dried, crusted dirt. Only a small stream of water flowed in the bottom of the channel about two feet wide. The dam he had seen over a month ago must have been why there was hardly any water in the branch he had found. That didn't seem fair to the other ranchers who also depended on the creek to water their land and livestock.

Three miles from where he had entered the creek bed, the stream turned to the west. The moon was up now and he could see a few trees bunched to his right so he rode that way, hoping he could find a place to camp. Before he got to the trees, the soil turned softer; he could hear his horse's hooves squish on wet ground. There must be a spring close by, seeping out of the ground. He turned the horse enough to get out of the water and dismounted at the edge of the trees.

Oliver set up camp away from the wet ground and tethered his horse so he couldn't go far.

The following morning, he built a small fire for coffee and was drinking some when he heard chains rattle. A wagon with two men came along the creek bank but stopped two hundred yards from where he was. It looked like they were doing something in the creek bed, so Oliver went ahead and finished his coffee before he saddled his horse and gathered his things. He knew better, but he wanted to talk to another human. It had been a month since he'd interacted with anyone besides the two men he killed on the range.

When he rode toward them, the men, one older and the other a young man of about fifteen, stopped what they were doing and watched him. "Howdy, I'm Canyon. I camped over by that spring last night. I'm just riding through and saw y'all working."

"Do you work for Paul Gaines?" asked the older man.

"No, sir. I've never met the man."

"Canyon, that's an odd name. Is it your first or last name?"

"It's just Canyon." This was the second time he had used his middle name, and it worked.

"I'm curious, what are you doing?" asked Canyon.

"The creek is about to dry up, and we're building a dam across the creek bed to trap what little water is flowing through my land. My cows require water to survive," said the older man.

"Is this the same creek that flows through the range on the Gaines Ranch?" asked Canyon.

"Yep, it is. This creek used to have plenty of water for everyone until Gaines did something to the stream so he could starve out all the smaller ranchers," said the man.

Canyon dismounted, walked to the two men, and stuck out his hand. "What are your names?"

"I'm Bartholomew Wotton, and this is my grandson, Isaiah Wotton. You can call me Bart."

"It's nice to meet you. I hate to tell you this, but Gaines has built a large dam across the creek and formed a tank that probably covers thirty acres."

"That no-good polecat," said Bart in a disgusted tone. "I knew something was wrong."

"Grandpa, what will we do about it?" asked Isaiah.

"There ain't much we can do about it. We can't set foot on Gaines's range, or he'll have his men kill us."

"I'll tell you what I think," said Canyon. "How about I help you build the dam, and then we cut a ditch from that spring up where those willows are and let that water run into the tank?"

Bart looked toward the willows and smiled. "That's a good idea, but I can only pay you a little. We're a shoe-string outfit, and I ain't got much money."

"You give me a place to lay my head and a few meals, and I'll help you out," said Canyon.

The three men spent the rest of the day working with picks and shovels, building an embankment across the stream. When they left at the end of the day, about six inches of water was in the bottom of the brook. When Canyon first saw the creek it was just a trickle of water moving down the stream, hardly enough for one cow.

CHAPTER THIRTEEN

Canyon, Isaiah, and Bart were on their way to the Wotton house when Canyon asked, "Bart, do you have a plow or something similar that we can use to loosen up the ground for the ditch? It'll make the shovel work much easier and quicker. I also think we should cut those willow trees down. All they do is suck up water that you want to run into the tank."

"Yep, I have a breaking plow and a strong team of mules. It's a good idea to do that, and you're right about them willows. They ain't good for nothing. We'll load the wagon in the morning with all the necessary tools."

"We may be able to clean the spring so it'll produce more water," said Canyon.

"That would be nice. Me and Isaiah have dug one tank over at another location that is spring fed, but it's almost dry from the summer heat. So we could sure use any water that comes our way."

"To be honest, I have yet to learn about cattle or how a ranch operates. I was raised in the city and worked on steam-powered riverboats."

"Are you any good with that gun you carry?" asked Bart.

"I'm still alive. Does that answer your question?"

"I reckon so. I'm not one to carry a gun. I have a rifle and a shotgun that we use for hunting, but that's all. It's been my experience that a gun can get a feller killed if he came across the wrong person. That's what happened to my boy, Isaiah's pa."

"I'm sorry to hear that, but I'm not your son, and I'll keep my gun handy if that's okay with you. Who killed your son?"

Bart slapped the back of his team with the bridle reins. "It was Jeff Gaines. They had words in town one night about six months back, and he called my boy out, knowing he wasn't a gunfighter. Jeff shot him three times."

"Like I said, I'm sorry about your son. You probably don't know this, but Jeff Gaines came against someone much faster than him in the saloon in town. He's dead and won't ever kill again."

Bart stopped the team and looked at Canyon. "Are you sure about that? Jeff is mighty fast from what I hear."

"Yeah, Jeff is dead."

"Who killed him?"

"Just some feller passing through."

"I bet old Paul is fit to be tied," said Bart. "He thought that the sun rose and set on that boy."

"Probably so. Why would Gaines dam up the creek and hoard all the water?"

"He's trying to starve out the small spreads so he can have all the free range in these parts. If we don't have water, we're out of business."

"That doesn't seem right. I reckon you'll just have to get your own water," said Canyon.

Canyon could see the house and outbuildings in the distance now and assumed it was where the Wotton family lived. There were five large trees scattered around the yard to provide shade. The house was built out of rough-sawn planks and had never seen paint. The roof was made from cedar shakes. The back of the house had a small porch that shielded the back door. Twenty feet to the left of the door was the water well. This meager residence was the total opposite of the hacienda on the Gaines Ranch. The barn and other outbuildings looked the same as the house, with unpainted boards and shake roofs.

Canyon dismounted by the corral made out of poles tied to posts and removed his horse's saddle. "I'll get the rails down for you, Mr. Canyon, so you can put your pony in the lot," said Isaiah.

"Thanks. Can I put my saddle and gear in the barn?"

"Yes, sir, there is a saddle horse inside the door."

After Canyon came out of the barn from stowing his things, he helped Bart and Isaiah unhook the wagon and put the horses in the corral.

"Come to the house. You can use our water well out back to wash up before supper," said Bart, who then turned to Isaiah. "Son, go tell your sister we have one more mouth to feed, so she'll have plenty cooked."

"Yes, sir. I'll be right back."

Canyon and Bart had already finished washing their hands and faces when Isaiah came out with a towel they could use to dry off with. "Brenda said supper will be ready in twenty minutes."

"Thanks, son," said Bart. "Come on, Canyon, and I'll introduce you to my granddaughter while Isaiah draws a couple of buckets of water for the kitchen."

They entered the kitchen through the back door, and

when he saw the girl, Canyon was surprised. He assumed that the granddaughter would be close to Isaiah's age, but she was more his own age in the early twenties. "Brenda, this is our new hand. He's going to help us out around here for a while. His name is Canyon."

Brenda stuck out her hand, and Canyon took it in his hand while looking into the prettiest hazel eyes he had ever seen.

"Miss Brenda, the pleasure is all mine. It's so nice to meet you."

She blushed and tried not to smile. "It's nice to meet you also, Mr. Canyon."

"Let's go out on the porch and sit while she finishes up with supper," said Bart.

When the two men sat down, Canyon asked. "How many heads of cattle do you have on your place?"

"Probably around a thousand to twelve hundred head. It's been two years since I've been able to take any to market, which has increased the herd in size. It's just Isaiah and me to make a drive, and I don't want to leave Brenda here by herself. I don't have the money to hire cowhands to help us. I've been fortunate to sell a few heads throughout the year to some of the neighbors. We've also driven a few at a time to Abilene."

Brenda came to the door. "Supper is ready. You all come on in."

Brenda reached out her hand to Canyon and Bart when they were all seated.

Canyon didn't know what was happening until Bart prayed. "Lord, thank you for this day and for the food that we have. Bless our family and our new friend. Amen."

Brenda passed bowls of food around the table. The conversation was light until they finished, and she passed around a blackberry cobbler. Canyon hadn't eaten this good in over a month.

When he finished his cobbler, he said, "I appreciate the fine food. It was delicious. Do you want me to help with the dishes?"

"No, that's Isaiah's job. You go talk to Grandpa and rest," said Brenda.

Canyon and Bart went back out to the porch and sat down. "You ain't used to saying grace over your meals, are you?" asked Bart.

"No, I'm not. That was a first for me. I'm not religious, but I read the Bible when I was younger."

"Just so you know, we pray at every meal, and Sunday is a day of rest unless it's an emergency. We also have a Bible study on Sunday mornings. I don't cotton to foul language or being around drunkards."

"I'm glad you told me that. Of course I'll abide by your customs. And I'm not one to drink, but I'm also not one to turn the other cheek to my enemies."

Bart sat staring out at the yard; then he turned to Canyon. "Tell me the truth, did you kill Jeff Gaines?"

"My name is Oliver Canyon Golden, and yes, I'm the man who killed Jeff. I stopped him when he was getting ready to hit one of the saloon girls. He called me out and drew first. I killed him in self-defense, and the local marshal told me to leave town. Paul has his hired guns looking for me, but they don't know what I look like, and they sure don't know I'm going by the name Canyon. If you want me to leave, I'll ride out first thing in the morning."

Bart wiped tears from his eyes. "I may be a Christian, but you have no idea how many times I have prayed for Jeff to get his due. So no, sir, you're welcome here, but I want to keep this conversation between us."

"I'm fine with that, and if it's okay with you, I'll head

to the barn and fix myself a nice bed of hay to sleep on. I'll see you in the morning."

"You go get your rest. We have a hard day's work ahead of us tomorrow," said Bart, who got out of his chair and went inside his house while Canyon walked away.

CHAPTER FOURTEEN

Canyon had the best night's sleep he'd had in a month and woke up refreshed. He was thankful for the soft bed of hay on which he had laid his bedroll. It was much better than the rock shelf he used in the box canyon. The water well was his first stop, where he poured a bucket full of cool water on his head. As he shook the water out of his hair, the realization of how long his hair had grown since his last haircut hit him. He pushed the lengthy locks out of his eyes.

He returned to the barn and rummaged through his bag until the comb was uncovered. After tidying himself up, he went to the back door of the house, now presentable for Brenda. That brought a smile to the young man's face. She wasn't the prettiest girl he had ever seen, but the attraction was there for him, and he hoped for her as well.

Brenda was setting food on the table when Canyon knocked on the back screen door. "Come on in, Canyon. You don't have to knock."

"I think it's only polite that I knock before entering."

"The cups are on the table, so go ahead and help yourself to coffee. You can sit where you did last night."

"Thanks. Do you need any help with breakfast?" Canyon asked.

"No, I have it under control. You drink your coffee."

Canyon did as she said and sat down to sip the hot liquid. He couldn't help but watch as she finished cooking and put the food on the table. When everything was prepared, Brenda hollered out so the others would hear. "Breakfast is ready!"

Canyon started to reach for a platter of cathead biscuits, but Brenda reached out and touched his hand. "You have to wait until Grandpa blesses the food."

"Sorry, I forgot. Everything sure looks delicious. I think you're trying to spoil me with all this food."

She smiled and kept her hands in her lap until Bart and Isaiah had sat down. Then she reached out, took Canyon's hand and gave it a squeeze before taking her grandpa's hand while he said a prayer.

Bart was a lot more talkative at the table this morning. "We need to gather up the plow and a couple more shovels. Is there anything else either of you can think of that we'll need out there?"

"If we're going to cut down those trees, we'll need saws and an axe," said Canyon.

"How about loading the dirt from the ditch into the back of the wagon and unloading it on top of the dam?" asked Isaiah.

"That's a good idea. Isaiah, you fill the canteens at the well while me and Canyon harness up the team to the wagon. The two horses that pull the wagon can pull the plow, especially since it's not very far."

Brenda put her fork down on her plate and took a drink from her coffee cup. "Grandpa, I hate to give you bad news, but we must stock up on provisions soon. I'm almost out of flour, meal, and a few other things."

Bart didn't say anything, just kept eating. No one said anything until he finished his food and pushed his plate forward so he could set his coffee cup in its place. "I reckon we'll have to figure out how to take some of the cows to Abilene."

"I have an idea," said Brenda. "I'll drive the wagon, and the three of you can herd the cattle. That way I'm not here alone, and with all of us going, we can take more cows."

Bart took another swallow of coffee. "That just might work. We have to finish the ditch at the spring first, and then we can gather up thirty or forty heads to take to market."

Canyon finished eating before he said, "I can use a shovel and help with the ditch, but I don't know how to use that plow, and I sure don't know how to herd cattle."

Brenda looked at Canyon and smiled. "Maybe you should drive the wagon, and I'll help with the cows."

Isaiah burst out laughing, and so did Bart. "What's so dad-blasted funny? I can ride a horse," said Brenda.

Isaiah pointed his finger at his sister. "You need to stick with cooking and cleaning and let the men herd cattle. I remember the last time you helped, and we chased cows for two days."

"You hush your smart mouth, little brother. I can herd cattle as good as anyone," said Brenda.

"We have to finish with our water project first, and then we'll plan out the trip to Abilene," said Bart, and stood up. "Canyon, if you're done, let's get busy."

Once the plow and other tools were in the wagon, Canyon rode his horse and Isaiah rode on the wagon with Bart to the spring. Bart and Isaiah went to work with the plow, harrowing out the ditch while Canyon cut down the smaller willow trees. He managed all of them except one, for which he would need another person to help with the two-man crosscut saw.

By late afternoon they had the ditch plowed and were spreading the loose dirt out on the dam. Bart sat down on the back of the wagon. "I'm bushed. What say we go back to the house and start back tomorrow?"

Canyon kept shoveling the dirt from the ditch. "How about we concentrate on opening the ditch and let the water flow tonight? We can haul the rest of the dirt tomorrow and cut down the last tree."

"That's fine by me," said Isaiah. "Grandpa, you rest for a little while, and me and Canyon will open up the ditch."

"Isaiah, you take that grubbing hoe and get the loose dirt from the ditch, and I'll work on cleaning out the spring and removing the last of the dirt between it and the channel," said Canyon.

By the time it was dark, water flowed into the tank they had built from the spring. It wasn't a big stream, but it would help fill the tank over time so the cattle could have more water.

Brenda had supper on the table when the men finally came to the house to eat. There was little conversation since everyone was worn out from the hard day's work. After supper, Canyon went to the barn and fell into a deep sleep.

CHAPTER FIFTEEN

The following morning, the men were back at the spring. Canyon and Isaiah went to work on the last tree with the saw while Bart loaded the wagon with dirt. There was already a foot of water in the tank, and with the trees cut down, they hoped for more. They finished up their grueling task as the sun set in the west that evening. It was difficult for the three worn-out men to load the plow in the bed of the wagon since they were so tired from the day's work.

As everyone finished eating supper that night, Bart drank the last of his coffee and put the cup down on the table. "In the morning, the three of us will go to the south range and start moving cattle toward the house. I'm hoping we can round up close to fifty head for this trip. If this works out, maybe we can do it again in a few weeks."

"When do you think we can get started to Abilene?" asked Brenda.

"Maybe the day after tomorrow," said Bart. "Brenda, you can help with the herd if you ride a horse. We can also bring a couple of packhorses to carry provisions for the trip and to bring our supplies back."

"That would be great if we could make another drive in a couple of weeks. Especially since we now have four riders to keep the cows moving," said Isaiah.

"Then that's settled," said Bart. "Tomorrow, Canyon, Isaiah, and I will start gathering the cows, and Brenda can start putting together rations for the trip. I suspect we can be in Abilene in three days."

Canyon lay awake on his bed that night, staring at the barn's roof. He was happy that he had stopped to help Bart out a few days ago at the spring, and even though the work he was doing was hard, it was fulfilling to know that it meant something to this family. Water for the cattle was essential, and he would get to begin his education as a cowboy tomorrow.

Then a thought came to him. God had sent him a message when he'd had that dream more than two weeks ago. Was this going to be his new life away from the poker table and the violence that came with it? That question ran through his mind until he drifted off to sleep.

Canyon arrived for breakfast early to give himself a chance to be alone with Brenda. While sipping his coffee, he said, "What do you like to do when you're not cooking or cleaning?"

She looked at him and raised one eyebrow. "I enjoy riding on the range. I used to like to fish when the creek was full. I also crochet pretty things. What do you like to do, Canyon?"

He had to think for a few seconds. "I enjoy playing cards, and I like to see new places."

"Are you a gambler?"

"Yes, I am. Why do you ask?"

"When I hold your hand while Grandpa prays, it's

soft and smooth. That makes me think you haven't done much manual work."

Canyon looked at his hands and smiled. "I swept and mopped floors on the riverboats until I was nineteen. That's where I learned to play cards. I studied the players' facial expressions and body language and learned how to play the percentages in my spare time. I saved my money and started gambling when I was nineteen. That's what I've done until I stopped to help Bart and Isaiah on the tank dam. I'm trying hard to find a less violent profession."

"I see. Does that mean that you've killed men?"

"Let's change the subject and talk about something more pleasant," said Canyon.

"Okay. Are you excited to learn to be a cowboy?"

"Actually, I am. It's something that I need in my life right now. I'm tired of my former life and ready for a change."

Bart and Isaiah entered the kitchen, and Canyon quit talking about wanting to change his life. This time he waited until Bart had finished praying before he filled his plate. Bart wasn't one to talk and eat, which was okay with Canyon.

Isaiah asked, "Do you think we'll need our chaps today for gathering the cattle?"

Bart waited until he swallowed his food. "I suspect those cows will most likely be in the mesquites, and we don't want to take a chance of getting stuck by thorns. Canyon, there's an extra pair hanging up in the tack room that you can use."

Canyon nodded.

"Grandpa, where on the range are you going to look for the cattle, in case I want to come and help?"

"We'll go south to the old tank that we dug. From there, we may want to drive the herd closer to the new tank. I'm almost sure the one that the cows have been using is practically dry. If you want to come with us, I'll saddle your horse."

"Fine. I'll wash the dishes and come outside."

After the men finished breakfast, they saddled their mounts, and as Canyon came out of the barn wearing chaps for the first time in his life, he saw Brenda coming from the house. She wore britches, a shirt, a hat, and sheepskin chaps. He wanted to wave at her but thought it might be too forward, and he didn't want to offend her or Bart.

The four riders headed south and after a half mile, Bart pointed to the west. A herd of about two hundred cattle was grazing on the tall grass. "What kind of grass are they eating?" asked Canyon.

"It's a mixture of big bluestem and Indian grass, but there could also be some little bluestem around here. Over west is mostly buffalo grass. It doesn't grow as tall. Let's ride to the old tank and see how it looks, then we'll start moving the cows," said Bart.

The tank was almost dry except for an area about ten feet in diameter. Canyon could see where the cows had been walking in the mud to get water. The spring that supplied water to the tank was still running a small stream, but the cows were drinking more than it could provide.

"We'll spread out on the other side of the herd and start them walking toward the new tank. Don't overwork your horses, otherwise they'll quit on you. We have all day to get them there," said Bart.

"Come with me, Canyon, and I'll show you what to do," said Brenda.

They rode to the far west side of the herd. "Stay close to me, and we'll start them going east. You'll have to whoop and holler to get their attention, but don't crowd the ones with horns too much. We don't want one to gore your horse."

Canyon saw that Bart and Isaiah both had ropes about eight foot long and were hitting the back ends of the cattle with them, getting the animals to move. "I have a short piece of rope in my bag. Will that help?" said Canyon.

"Yes, that will help. When we get this group moving, you and I will put some distance between us so the cattle stay bunched. Once we separate, you'll have to watch both sides of you to make sure none of the cows try to hang back. If they do, then you'll have to go after them. Watch what I do, and you can do the same. If you have a bandana, you may want to tie it across your mouth and nose to keep the dust out."

It took them a good hour until they had the cattle trailing and heading toward the new tank. Suddenly the wind changed direction and began to gust from the west. Bart left the herd, rode west, and sat gazing at the sky for a few seconds before going to each rider in turn. "Go to the house. There's a storm coming," he said to Canyon.

All four riders urged their mounts to run back to the house. "Put the horses in the barn and leave them saddled," said Bart. "This storm may not last long. If we can, we'll go back to the herd once it's passed. Brenda, you go on to the house and make coffee."

The three men were walking toward the house when it began to sprinkle, and they started running as fast as they could.

Fortunately, the sky waited to open up until they were inside, and then it poured down rain.

"Hallelujah, this rain will fill up the tanks, and the cows will have plenty of water for a while," said Brenda.

"Yes, and it will settle the dirt so we don't have to eat so much dust when we drive the cows to Abilene," said

Isaiah. "I'm thankful for the rain. I wasn't looking forward to being swallowed up in dust for three days."

The rain continued for over an hour, and then it went away and left the countryside shadowed with cloudy skies. Bart went outside to look around, and when he came back in, he said, "Let's mount up and see how bad the herd has scattered. The ground is wet and soggy, so we'll take it slow with the horses. We sure don't want one to go down."

Canyon went inside the barn and found a longer rope to slap the cows with, and the riders started toward where they had left the herd.

The cattle were in the same general vicinity, and all the riders had to do was bunch them back up. Within an hour, the herd was again heading east. Canyon got the hang of riding back and forth at the back of the drive, keeping the cows moving by using the rope and whooping at them.

When he saw the tank, Canyon couldn't believe his eyes. The tank was full of water; some even had gone over the spillway they had made. Water came down the creek that fed the pond, and the heavy rain had caused enough runoff to help too.

Bart and Isaiah rode to Canyon and Brenda at the back of the herd. "You two stay here, and Isaiah and I will start cutting out the cattle we'll take to market. Then, as we make them leave the main herd, the two of you will take them to the other side of that hill." He pointed in the direction where he wanted them to go.

Brenda and Canyon sat on their mounts and waited until six heads of cattle came toward them. Brenda took the rear while Canyon kept the cows from turning back toward the herd. After a short time, many steers and older cows were going toward the barn where they would be kept in a small meadow until they started them toward Abilene.

Canyon was tired but also proud that he was learning a new skill. He looked forward to the trail drive to Abilene; he could get a haircut there and buy new duds and boots. Unfortunately, the low-top boots he had been wearing were not meant for cowboys.

CHAPTER SIXTEEN

The men went to the barn the following morning after they had finished an early breakfast. Canyon and Bart saddled the riding horses while Isaiah entered the horse pen and caught the two packhorses. Brenda already had most of the supplies they would use during the trip in gunnysacks, ready for easy transport.

"Isaiah, when you finish with the pack saddles, take both of the animals to the house and help your sister load our food and bedding. You be sure and tie everything on so it doesn't come loose," said Bart.

"Yes, sir. Do you want me to bring your hunting rifle?" asked Isaiah.

"No, Canyon has a gun if we need one. Go on and help your sister get loaded. We're burning daylight."

The cattle didn't want to move that morning, and the riders needed help getting them to start north. Bart found an older bull and made him go to the front of the herd so the rest would follow him. By noon they had only traveled three miles.

Canyon was riding drag and had to work his horse hard to keep the cows moving forward.

Bart rode to the flank and started slapping the cows with his rope in hopes that they would walk faster. When he was close to Canyon, he said, "You trade places with Isaiah so you can rest your horse. We'll wear our mounts out if we don't rest them."

Canyon could barely hear the older man over the cows' hooves hitting the ground and all the bawling. He waved his hand in acknowledgment and moved his horse to the swing position, hollering out to Isaiah, "Bart wants you to go help with the drag."

Isaiah nodded and turned to the back of the herd.

There wasn't as much dust from the cows' hooves riding the swing. Canyon would have to turn a cow occasionally, but this position allowed his horse to rest.

They didn't stop to camp until it was almost dark. The location they chose provided an abundance of grass but no water. Canyon asked, "What are we going to do about water? Won't they need some before we get to Abilene?"

"Yep, they're thirsty, but it's okay for a day or two. This grass has some moisture in it, and it will get them by for tonight. Tomorrow we'll go by a natural tank, and they can get their fill from it."

When camp was set up and Brenda was cooking, Bart, Isaiah, and Canyon sat on the ground drinking coffee. "One of us will have to keep the cows bunched tonight," said Bart. "Isaiah, you take the first watch, and Canyon can spell you at midnight."

"What exactly do I need to do?" asked Canyon.

"Basically, ride circles around the herd. If some of them start getting too far out, you'll make them go back to the rest of their friends. I'll spell you about four so you can get a few hours of shut-eye."

"I'll go ahead and get some sleep after supper, and when I relieve Isaiah, I'll do it all night," said Canyon.

"Okay, but if you get tired, come and wake me up.

You should ride Brenda's horse for a few hours and give your horse a rest. You worked him mighty hard today."

"I can do that. I'm sure that will help him tomorrow."

After supper, Canyon spread his bedroll by a tree and fell asleep. When he woke up, the moon was big and bright. A quick glance at his pocket watch indicated that it was ten minutes after midnight and time to put his saddle on Brenda's horse. Isaiah was easy to find on the west edge of the herd, just sitting on his horse watching the cows.

"Isaiah, how's it going?" asked Canyon.

"Really well. I haven't had to do much with them. They've been content with the grass where they're at."

"Good. You go on back to camp and get some rest."

Canyon stayed with the cows for a few hours and only had to turn a few. He came into camp at four and changed horses so Brenda's mount could eat grass and rest. While in camp, he put more wood on the hot coals for her to use to make coffee and cook breakfast when she got up.

"Canyon, are you having to push many of the cows back to the herd?" asked Bart. Canyon thought he'd been asleep, so the old man's voice surprised him.

"No, sir, the cattle are staying bunched and I'm just watching them eat."

"Go ahead and get some sleep. They'll be fine until we head out in a few hours."

"Thanks, Bart. I could use a little rest." After the long day of herding cattle, the wounds he'd received when he'd been shot over a month ago were a little sore, but he didn't want Bart to know.

Canyon lay down and fell off to sleep. He came awake with something brushing against his cheek. Startled, he swatted at what he thought was an insect and opened his eyes to see Brenda's smiling face. She had a blade of grass in her hand. "Wake up, sleepyhead, and come eat."

Canyon wanted to reach out to her but didn't. "You know that I'll get you back for that," he said as he got up. She said nothing as she waited for him to get up. They walked to the campfire, where Canyon filled his plate and sat down on the ground to eat.

"The herd will most likely be ready to go once we're packed up. They're thirsty and should take to the trail easier than yesterday," said Bart.

"Grandpa, I counted sixty-eight heads last night while I was night hawking," said Isaiah.

"That's good. I hope we get at least ten dollars a head out of them," said Bart.

Canyon finished eating and began to gather up his bedding and saddle his horse. Brenda came by while he was tying his bedroll to the back of his saddle and put her hand in the middle of his back and gave it a little rub.

"Be careful, and don't eat too much dust." She handed him a clean rag to put over his nose and mouth.

"Thanks, this will come in handy today. I'm sure it'll get really dusty back behind the herd."

She walked a couple of steps, then turned back toward him and said while walking back to him, "Hey, cowboy." She kissed him when he turned his head toward her and then she walked to her horse.

Canyon stood there red-faced with a blank look on his face. She might like him after all. He grinned, took his hat and knocked the dust from his britches before he got into the saddle with a little more spunk than he had the day before.

The cattle took to the trail with minimum difficulty that morning, and right before noon, they picked up the pace and walked faster. In fact, the ones in the lead were almost running. Brenda rode to the rear where Canyon was and said, "The cattle smells the water and are ready for a drink. All you have to do is follow along. You might want to slack back or move to the side and get out of this dust for a while."

"I think I'll do that and follow you."

Another ten minutes, and the lead cattle was belly-deep in the tank sucking up water. The pond was large enough that the cattle had no issue entering the pool. Canyon rode away from the herd and dismounted to wash off his face. He wanted to get as much dirt removed as possible. A short time later, the cattle began to turn away from the water and graze on the grass.

Bart waved his arms to signal everyone to get in position. Then he went to the front of the herd to ride point until the cows realized their journey wasn't over.

Isaiah came to the rear with Canyon since the tank was on the side where he rode the swing and wasn't needed there until the cattle cleared the area where the pond was located. They had to keep after the cattle, hollering and hitting them with their ropes until they started around the tank and headed north toward Abilene.

The rest of the day went well, and that night while they were eating supper, Bart said, "I figure we are within twelve miles of Abilene. We should arrive at the stock pens by tomorrow afternoon."

"That's good. I'm ready for a hot bath and some clean clothes," said Canyon.

The others laughed at his remarks, but he figured they were thinking the same thing.

Riding nighthawk that night went well for Isaiah and Canyon. The herd was small enough that they didn't have to turn many back during the night.

CHAPTER SEVENTEEN

The cattle pens at the Abilene stockyards came into view at two in the afternoon. Bart rode ahead and talked to a cattle buyer, while the rest of them stayed behind with the herd and pushed them on toward their destination. Five cowboys who worked at the pens opened two big double gates, and Canyon, Isaiah, and Brenda kept the cattle going toward the opening. Three of the wranglers who worked at the pens came out to help on their horses also.

The man Bart had been talking to entered a small shack of an office while Bart returned to the herd. The convenient way the holding pens were situated helped Canyon and the others get the cattle into them, where they would be kept until they were sent off to be butchered.

Canyon, Brenda, and Isaiah stayed on their mounts after the cattle were penned while Bart went inside to sign a bill of sale and collect his money.

As they waited, Brenda asked, "Do you know where we can bathe?"

Isaiah shook his head no.

But Canyon said, "I'm sure the barber shop has probably got a bathtub, and so does the hotel. With the railroad coming through here, there could also be a business owned by a Chinaman with a bath and laundry service."

Bart returned, smiling from ear to ear. "We sold sixty-eight head at thirteen dollars apiece. I think we should get hotel rooms, buy new clothes, and take a hot bath before eating supper at the café."

Brenda was the first one to speak up. "I'm ready to wash the grime off me and change into some nice clean clothes!"

Bart made arrangements at the Shady Brook Hotel for four rooms and hot baths for everyone. He was informed that the hotel had two rooms in which they could bathe.

Canyon told the others, "I'm going to the dry goods store and buy me some new clothes and a pair of boots. I'll take a bath at the barbershop when I get a shave and haircut."

Bart tried to give him money, but Canyon refused to take it.

"I don't need any money," said Canyon, since he had plenty.

With his new clothes in a package and the new boots on his feet, Canyon entered the barber shop and sat down. There was someone in the chair getting his hair cut. The man looked familiar, but he couldn't place where he knew him from. When the barber finished up and removed the apron from the man's lap, Canyon saw the tied-down holster that the man was wearing, and it dawned on him who he was. He suspected it was the ramrod of Paul Gaines's hired gunman. The tied-down gun reminded Canyon of the man he'd seen the night Paul had collected Jeff's body. Canyon didn't acknowledge the man but sat in the chair minding his own business, and waited until the barber was finished.

The gunfighter got up from the barber chair, looked at himself in the mirror, and paid the barber.

"Thanks, Mr. Chandler. You come back anytime," said the barber.

Chandler stopped when he was even with Canyon's chair. "Are you new around here, or just passing through?"

Canyon stood up, kept his right hand close to his gun, and tapped the holster with his index finger. "I'm new to Abilene and work on a ranch southeast of here."

"Who do you work for?" asked Chandler.

Canyon was already tired of all the questions and decided to see how far Chandler wanted to go with them. "That's none of your business, and if you go for that gun, I'll kill you right here in the barbershop."

Chandler started to laugh. "A little testy, aren't you? I was just being social. They call me Chandler. What's your name?"

Canyon kept his right hand by his gun, continued tapping the holster with his finger, and said, "I'm Canyon, and it's nice to make your acquaintance."

"I'll be seeing you around," said Chandler, and he left the barber shop.

Canyon sat down in the barber chair. "I want a shave, haircut, and a hot bath."

"Yes, sir, I'll get your water on to heat and then get busy with the shave. You sit here, and I'll be right back."

Canyon noticed that the barber's hands were shaking from what he guessed was fear. It was good that he was heating the water first to give him time to settle down so those shaking hands didn't cut him with the straight razor.

When the barber returned, Canyon said, "Cut my hair first. I don't want you slicing my face with those trembling hands."

"I'm sorry, but you probably don't know who Chandler is."

"I know exactly who he is. The issue is, he doesn't know who I am."

"You know he's a gunfighter who works for the Gaines Ranch?"

"Yes, I do, and he doesn't scare me. Now, stop the talking and calm down so I don't leave here with cuts all over my face," said Canyon.

With his hair cut, face shaved, and having had a hot bath, Canyon felt like a different man. His new clothes fit perfectly and made him feel more presentable for Brenda. He paid his bill and started to his hotel room with his old clothes under his arm. On the way there, he passed a laundry house and asked if they could wash his soiled clothing and have it ready by the morning. The little Asian woman spoke broken English but assured him his things would be prepared early the next day.

Brenda was sitting in the lobby of the hotel when he returned. She stood up and met him in the middle of the large room. "Well, don't you clean up mighty good, handsome?" She put her hand on his arm and gave him a little tug. "Turn around so I can see the rest of you."

"Stop it, or I may have to take matters into my own hands," said Canyon.

She stepped closer to him. "I double-dog dare you to do something," she said, never smiling, but he could see the hint of a smile as she raised one eyebrow.

He reached out and pulled her to him, put his lips against hers, and felt her tense up. The kiss lingered for a few seconds until he felt her body relax. "I accept your dare," he said when they parted.

"You sure did, and I like it. Come sit with me while we wait for Grandpa and Isaiah."

"Sure," said Canyon, and they sat down together on a

plush couch. "I must say that you look adorable yourself, Miss Brenda. And if I may be so bold, your lips tasted mighty good."

She was about to say something when Bart and Isaiah entered the lobby wearing their new clothes. "It looks like everyone is feeling better after getting cleaned up. Let's go eat," said Bart.

They were walking down the boardwalk with Bart and Isaiah in front and Brenda and Canyon following when Canyon saw Chandler come out of a store and lean against a porch post, watching them. He stood where he was until they were within six feet of his position.

"Hello, Wotton. I hear you sold a small herd of cattle in town today."

"I don't think it's any of your business what I do," said Bart.

Chandler pointed his finger at Bart. "I'm going to go check the brands on those cows, and if I find one Rocking G cow in the herd, then me and you are going to have problems."

Canyon walked forward to stand between Bart and Isaiah. "You make one more threat against my boss, and you'll answer to me," said Canyon, standing confidently, tapping his holster with his index finger.

"So, we meet again, whoever you are. I let that pass earlier at the barbershop, but you're beginning to get my dander up. I advise you to back off and go somewhere else to work," said Chandler.

Canyon smiled. "I know who you are and how fast you can pull iron, but you have no idea who I am or how fast I can pull this gun and kill you where you stand. Now you've made threats and started this show. What are you going to do?"

Chandler smiled and shook his head. "You have me there—I don't know who you are. But this happens to be your lucky day. I'm going to walk across the street this time, but the next time you call me out, you better be ready to pull leather." The hired gunman pulled himself away from the porch post he'd been leaning against and crossed the street.

Bart said, "Come on, it's over. Let's go eat."

"Y'all go ahead," said Canyon, never taking his eyes off Chandler. "I'll make sure he doesn't change his mind and try to shoot me in the back."

"Come on with us, Brenda," said Bart, taking her hand.

Canyon caught up with the rest of his party at the café. He sat at their table so that he could watch the street, in case Chandler or some other Gaines's hand wanted to try something.

After supper, they all returned to their hotel rooms, but Canyon stayed in the lobby to ensure they had no unwelcome visitors.

Around sundown, Brenda came back down to the lobby and sat beside him on the divan. "Canyon, would you have drawn against that awful man today?"

He reached out and took her hand. "I'll not idly stand by and watch the people I care for get mistreated by some bully. I'd have killed him today if he had gone for his gun."

"I know you would have. Deep down, you're a good, respectable man, but you are also one that won't be pushed around. Can I ask you a question?"

"Yes, and I'll tell you the truth."

"Did you kill Jeff Gaines?"

He looked her in the eye. "Yes, I killed Jeff in self-defense. He drew first but wasn't fast enough."

She smiled, but Canyon noticed there were tears forming in the corner of her eyes. "Thank you. I despised that man for what he did to our family. He killed our pa in cold blood." She put her arms around Canyon's neck and sobbed.

When she had regained her composure, Canyon said, "Come on, we need to get to sleep. I'll walk you to your room. Tomorrow will be a long day riding all the way home."

She put her arm in his as they started to the stairs.

Upon arriving at her room, he opened the door for her and touched her cheek. "I had fun this evening talking to you. Sweet dreams, pretty lady."

She went up on her tiptoes and kissed his cheek. "Good night, Canyon."

He stood in the hallway for a few seconds after she closed the door, and then went to his own room and sat at the window, watching the activity on the busy street.

Canyon wasn't sleepy yet, and the run-in with Chandler earlier in the afternoon had his anxiety up. He made sure he had some money in his pocket and eased his door open so it wouldn't wake the others. A few hands of poker would settle him down, and then he could rest.

CHAPTER EIGHTEEN

Canyon pushed through the swinging doors of the Silver Spur Saloon and stood there, letting his eyes adjust to the dim, smoke-filled room. This was one of the larger drinking establishments on the main street. He chose it because he had noticed the card tables through the window.

There were eight poker tables, and most of them were full of men playing cards. About twenty cowboys stood drinking at the L-shaped bar, which must have been imported from somewhere. Its top was sanded smooth and had some kind of finish on it that created a glare. Most saloons in the south and west had rough sawed oak bar tops, and only the ones that he had seen in the fancier places were like the one he saw. There was no large mirror behind the bar, which was strange. He thought there was probably a story behind it, but he wasn't going to ask today.

It was rumored that cowboys coming off a trail drive like to raise a ruckus and get rowdy. Maybe they had busted the mirror so many times that the saloon owner had quit putting it back up.

Canyon went through the area where the poker games were being played and wanted to be more impressed with what he saw. The games looked to be primarily low stakes, and the players were drinking a lot of whiskey. In addition, the saloon girls were catering to the players by sitting on their laps and getting them to buy more liquor. A poker game that involved too much rotgut whiskey usually ended in violence when some drunk cowboy lost his month's wage.

Canyon made his way to the bar and when the bartender looked his way, he pointed to the man next to him, who was drinking a beer, indicating that he wanted one also. While waiting on his drink, he placed his elbows on the bar top and watched the poker tables. The urge he'd had earlier to join in on a game was gone. Instead, he would drink his beer and go back to the hotel and get in bed.

The bartender returned and set a mug on the counter. Canyon turned and handed him the money for his drink. He picked up the mug, blew the foam off the top, and swallowed. Just as he put it back on the bar, something hit him in his kidneys so hard that his knees buckled, and the mug overturned, spilling the beer.

He tried to straighten up, but a driving fist hit him in his right temple, causing him to black out. When he regained his senses enough to realize what was happening, two men had their arms under his armpits and were dragging him across the room. His feet scraped across the sawdust that covered the floor, and the toes of his boots left tracks. He tried to jerk his arms free, but they wouldn't move.

He didn't remember going out the back door and into the alley. Next thing he knew, he regained consciousness again when someone doused him with a pan of water. One eye was having trouble focusing on the figure standing before him. He tried to lash out, but his arms were still being secured by the two assailants.

The man in front of him reached out and grabbed a handful of Canyon's hair and used it to lift his head so he could see who was talking to him.

It was Chandler. That figured, thought Canyon. He was unable to do anything, so he stayed slumped and let the two men hold him up.

Chandler slapped Canyon across the face, making him taste blood from the cuts on his lips. The men who beat him must have made him bleed.

"It looks like the ball is definitely in my court now, doesn't it?" said Chandler. "This is your one and only warning in life, gunslinger. I'm going to teach you a valuable lesson tonight."

Chandler wrapped his handkerchief around his knuckles. "Hold him up higher." The blows to Canyon's face and abdomen came one after the other.

Blood flowed from his nose and mouth. Both eyes swelled until they were almost shut, and he had gashes above them. He was only semiconscious and couldn't feel the pain like he had when they'd first hit him in the bar, but he could still hear the men's voices as they laughed at his demise.

"Drop him to the ground and hold on to his hands. I have one more surprise for him," said Chandler, laughing as he ground the heel of his boot into the back of both of Canyon's hands, tearing off chunks of skin. The helpless man screamed in pain and tried to jerk his outstretched arms back.

Then a boot hit him in the face, and darkness loomed up all around him.

CHAPTER NINETEEN

Bloodied and mangled, his entire body aching, Canyon woke up with a stabbing pain in his left cheek. It was then that he noticed he was in a bed. He tried to sit up, but it hurt too much. He couldn't see where he was because his eyes wouldn't open. He tried to make a fist but couldn't.

Someone pushed him back onto the bed. "Lie back down. I'm Dr. Reynolds. You've been beaten badly, and I'm trying to help."

It took a few seconds for the words to sink in. But after a moment he remembered getting attacked and beaten, and the doctor's words got through the haze in his mind. He lay back on the bed and let the sawbones work on him.

"What's your name?" asked the doctor.

"It's Canyon. What's your name?"

"I'm Dr. Mathias Reynolds. Now lie still. I'm going to put a bottle to your lips. Take a couple of swallows; it'll help with the pain. Then I'll tend to you the best that I can."

When Canyon woke up again, he could feel bandages on his eyes, face, and hands. "Doctor, are you here?"

"Yes, I'm here. You need to lie still and not reopen your wounds. Is there someone in town that I can notify about your condition?"

He had to think on that a minute since he wasn't in his right mind. "I'm here with Bart Wotton. He's at the hotel."

"Which hotel? We have more than one."

"Shady something, that's all I remember."

"That would be the Shady Brook Hotel. I'll have someone go there once it's daylight."

"What time is it?" asked Canyon.

"It's four in the morning. You've been here five hours. One of the girls at the saloon found you in the alley and thought you were dead."

"Why can't I see?"

"You were beaten so badly that your eyes are swollen shut. They'll be that way for a few days until I can get the swelling down."

"Doc, I hurt all over. What else did they do to me?"

"You probably have a concussion from the blows to your head. There's a deep gash on your left cheek. I think it's from a spur, by the look of the cut. I've sewn it shut with horsehair and put a poultice on it to fight infection. Your rib cage is bruised and most likely has a couple of cracked ribs. How long has it been since you were shot in the side?"

"That was a little over a month ago. Why do you ask?"

"I just happened to see it. It's healed nicely."

"Why are my hands bandaged?"

"Your attackers took their boots to your hands and scraped them up badly. I don't know if there are any broken bones or not. They'll be sore and painful for some time."

Canyon lay in deep sorrow at the news of his hands. They were so important to his card playing and for protection. What would he do if his hands were permanently damaged?

"Open your mouth. I have some laudanum to ease your pain," said the doctor, and put a bottle to Canyon's swollen lips so he could drink the liquid.

He tried to remember each man who beat him. The faces of his attackers were a blur except for one. Chandler had been there, talking to him and giving orders to his cronies. But what about the others? How many had there been? He could remember two men carrying him out of the saloon's back door and getting hit.

The medicine made his mouth so dry that he couldn't swallow. He tried to sit up again, but his muscles weren't working. Finally he called out, "Doctor, are you here?"

"What do you need? I'm right here."

"My mouth is so dry. Can I have water to drink?"

"Yes, I'll be right back."

He drank a full glass of water and drifted into unconsciousness.

CHAPTER TWENTY

Canyon woke up to voices in the room. He recognized Dr. Reynolds's voice, but the other voice was so broken up with sobs that he couldn't tell whose it was.

"Who's here?" he asked.

Dr. Reynolds said, "You have a couple of visitors. Mr. Wotton and his granddaughter are here to see you."

Canyon felt Brenda take hold of his arm above his wrist, and he put his other hand on hers. "I'm glad that you're here."

"Canyon, I'm so sorry that this happened to you. Do you know who did this terrible thing?"

"Yup, it was Chandler and two of his men."

"That figures. You made Chandler mad yesterday on the boardwalk," said Bart.

"Maybe that was it, or it could be that he wanted me out of the way so he could do something to your ranch. Bart, you need to load everyone up and go home. I have a bad feeling that Chandler will try something if you're not there," said Canyon.

"I'm staying here with you," said Brenda.

"No, you need to go home and help protect your property. I'll be fine here until I can ride."

Brenda started to sob again and squeezed his arm. "But I want to stay and take care of you."

"Please go with your grandpa. He's going to need you a lot more than I do. I'm terrified Chandler will try something with everyone gone."

"He's right. We need to get Isaiah and head on home. If there is no trouble for a few days, you can ride back to see how Canyon is doing."

Brenda blew her nose. "Okay, Grandpa, but I intend to hold you to your word about letting me come back to check on Canyon."

"I'll go get Isaiah, and you can stay here until we get the horses loaded with our supplies. Canyon, you do what the doctor says, and I'll see you later."

"Bart, would you get my travel bag out of my room and bring it to the doctor's office before you leave?" asked Canyon.

"I sure will," said Bart. "Is there anything else you need?"

"No, but you should buy yourself a gun. I'm afraid for your safety," said Canyon.

"No. Killing goes against my Christian beliefs, and I won't give in to violence. I appreciate your concern, but I have to do what I think is right," said Bart.

"Okay, just be careful, and don't go anywhere alone," said Canyon.

"I'll be back after we're loaded. Brenda, you be ready when we come back. I want to be home tonight," said Bart as he started to the door.

Brenda came closer and put her hand against Canyon's good cheek. "You feel a little warm; you might have a fever. I'm going to get a wet cloth and wash your face. There's still dried blood on it in places."

"Okay, thanks. I wish Bart would do more to protect you and Isaiah. I'm really concerned about what will happen."

Brenda began lightly washing away the blood, then leaned over and kissed his swollen lips. "I wish I could stay and care for you, but I understand your concerns." She leaned in and touched her lips to his for the second time. "I better get my sugars in before Grandpa gets back. He might frown on me loving you."

"Well, I'm glad you are. It makes me feel better," said Canyon. "As soon as I can ride, I'll head back to the ranch. This is not over with Chandler. He didn't beat me because I made him mad. He beat me because I'm a threat to him and the rest of the hired guns who work for Paul Gaines."

"You don't fret none about revenge just yet. You'll have plenty of time to do that when you're well from the beating," said Brenda as Canyon started breathing slower and his body relaxed from the laudanum.

He dozed off to sleep and was awakened by Brenda kissing him on the cheek. "I have to go. Grandpa just arrived. But I'll be back in a few days."

"Come closer and take my hand and lean down. I want to tell you something," said Canyon.

Brenda did as he asked and he whispered in her ear. "I really like you and want to be your beau."

"Hmm, I'll think about it," said Brenda, kissing his lips. Then she walked away and Canyon heard the door close.

A few minutes later, Dr. Reynolds returned to the room and said, "If you're in pain, I can give you another swallow of laudanum."

"I'm okay for now. Doctor, will I be able to use my hands again?"

"I don't rightly know. I can't tell yet if there is any

permanent damage. I'll do everything I can to get them working properly. You need to practice patience and let them heal."

"Thanks. I do believe that another swallow of that laudanum might help me take another nap."

CHAPTER TWENTY-ONE

The effects of the laudanum and the concussion kept the injured young man in a state of unconsciousness most of the remainder of the day, but he did stay awake long enough to drink chicken broth for supper that night. The doctor changed the bandages on his hands and applied new poultices to his eyes and the cut on his cheek.

"Doctor, can you tell if my hands are looking better yet?" asked the young gambler.

"No, but I believe the swelling has gone down some on your eyes. I hope that you'll be able to see in a day or two," replied the doctor.

Canyon drank more of the painkiller and sometime during the night, he opened his eyes to see a man dressed in black with a hood on his head standing beside the bed.

"Get away from me. I don't want to go with you." Canyon swung his bandaged hands at the dark figure, but he couldn't hit him because his hands kept going through the creature, like it was a ghost. He was so frustrated with his attempts that he finally lay back down, and the figure removed the hood from his head, but there wasn't anything there. No head or face, only open space.

Canyon screamed and sat up, only to be pushed back down, and then he heard a voice talking to him. "Canyon, you're delirious and have a fever," said Dr. Reynolds. "You must lie back down and quit trying to fight, or I'll have to tie your arms down."

"You mean I was dreaming everything I just saw?" asked Canyon in disbelief.

"Yes. You have a fever, and I'm going to give you a spoonful of quinine and another dose of laudanum and hope that helps with your temperature. With some luck, you can go back to sleep."

Canyon lay on the bed in his darkness, scared thinking about what the creature had looked like. After a few minutes, he saw his ma in the kitchen with Brenda scurrying around preparing supper, but when he reached out for her, she wasn't there. He couldn't believe that he couldn't touch her until he realized that it was just another dream, and he became at ease and slept.

When he finally woke up the following day, he felt much better and was hungry. "Dr. Reynolds, are you here?" he called out.

A woman said, "I'm Lucy, Dr. Reynolds's nurse. What can I do for you?"

"I'm thirsty and hungry. Can I have something to eat?"

"Let me ask the doctor. I'll be right back."

Lucy returned carrying a pitcher of water and a tall glass. "I'm going to help you sit up and put pillows behind your back and head so you can drink water."

"Thank you, I can sit up by myself."

"You probably can, but I'm going to help you anyway. On the count of three, you can help." She placed her hand under his back and counted. When she said three, she raised him to a sitting position with his help.

"Are you dizzy or sick to your stomach?" she asked.

"No, I feel okay right now."

She held the glass to his lips while he took gulps of water.

"This water tastes so good. What about something to eat?" he asked.

"The doctor said you're on a liquid diet of soup and soft foods that don't require chewing. You'll have to be careful and not chew for a few days since you have a sore jaw and stitches. I'm going to the café to see what they have that you can eat."

"Can I stay sitting up while you go after my food?"

"Sure. I'm leaving now, so you're in the room alone."

Lucy returned with soup and some runny mashed potatoes. She helped him eat until he said, "I've had enough for now. Can we give it a little time before I eat the rest?"

"Sure, you tell me when you're ready and I'll help you. In the meantime, I have work to do."

Thirty minutes later, Lucy helped Canyon drink down more of the chicken soup and spooned in the last of the creamy mashed potatoes. After he had eaten, he laid back down and slept.

Dr. Reynolds woke Canyon up by removing the poultices covering his eyes. "Canyon, open your eyes and tell me what you see."

Canyon tried to open his eyes, but they seemed stuck. "I can't, Doctor. They feel like they are sewn shut or something."

"Lucy, go get me a warm wet rag. I'll wash off your eyelids, Canyon. They look a little matted," said Dr. Reynolds.

The doctor gently blotted each eye with the wet cloth,

then used his thumb and index finger to pry the eyelid open. Canyon began to blink and said, "I can see. Not really good, but good enough to see y'all's faces."

"Good. I'm going to wash your eyes some more and remove the rest of the eye matter that's left," said Dr. Reynolds.

When the doctor finished, Canyon said. "That's much better, Doctor. I assume that they're still swollen by the way they feel."

"Yes, they are, but the swelling is going down. You rest now, and tomorrow we'll see about getting you out of this bed."

"That sounds good to me," said Canyon.

CHAPTER TWENTY-TWO

anyon got out of bed the following morning without any dizziness or nausea. The first thing he did was go to a mirror that hung on the wall over a table with a small wash bowl. The reflection showed a man he didn't recognize. Both eyes were still swollen, and the skin underneath them was black, blue, purple, and green. Even his nose was swollen. He wanted to see what was under the bandage on his cheek, but that would have to wait until the doctor removed the dressing.

He spent the rest of the day walking around his room. When he got tired, he lay down and napped, then got up and walked some more. Lucy brought him more soup and runny potatoes with gravy to eat.

That night when the doctor examined Canyon's injuries, he removed the bandage from his cheek. "Son, it's healing nicely but will leave a scar. I'm truly sorry, but I did the best I could."

"I want to see it." Canyon got up and went to the mirror. What he saw made him harbor a new indebtedness to Chandler. His hazel eyes were scarcely visible and his face was still filled with multiple-colored bruising. The scar on his cheek was three inches long and jagged. The bruising and swelling would disappear, but the scar would remain with him. Chandler and the two men who did this to him would pay with their lives.

Canyon came back to his bed and sat down. "Would it be all right if I went outside tomorrow and sat for a while?" he asked.

"I don't see why not. Getting some sun might do you a lot of good. Lucy will fix you a jar of water to take with you, and there's a chair out front on the porch of my office," said the doctor.

"I think out back in the alley would be best for a few days," said Canyon. "I'm in no shape to fight if someone wants to try and harm me some more."

"You're right. I'll have Lucy put a chair for you out back with your water."

"Thanks. Could I ask you one more favor?"

"Of course. What is it?"

"Remove the bandages on my hands. I have to see them," said Canyon.

"Okay. I want to see if you can move your fingers anyway, so we might as well do it today." The doctor asked Lucy, "Would you go heat some water? Don't get it too hot; I want him to soak his hands in it."

The doctor started on Canyon's right hand. When the bandage and poultice were removed, he said, "I'm surprised the swelling has decreased considerably and your hand looks much better. I'll get the other one unbandaged, then you can soak them in warm water to loosen the muscles."

Canyon raised both hands and looked at the bruised, scabbed flesh on the back side of his former well-manicured hands. They were his livelihood, and he needed them in order to survive. After turning them over to see his palms, Lucy set a pan of water on the bedside table where he could put both hands in it.

"You can begin to bend your fingers so we can see if they will work," said the doctor.

Canyon slowly started to flex and blend the digits on both hands.

"Do you feel any discomfort when you turn them?" asked the doctor.

"I don't feel pain. But I do feel a real tightness and some discomfort," said Canyon.

"Good. Now make a fist as tight as you can."

Canyon could make a fist, and then he relaxed his fingers and did it again. "Doctor, I think they will work fine in a few more days."

"I think so too. However, you must still be careful with your hands and not let them start bleeding again."

"I'll be extra careful. I need them to heal."

"I'll see you tomorrow," said Dr. Reynolds, and he left the room.

Canyon slept better that night, knowing his hands were healing and he would have full use of them in a few days or weeks.

The following morning after breakfast, he took a hot bath in the tub that the doctor had for patients and changed into clean clothes. It felt good to get cleaned up. While getting dressed, he remembered that he still had clothes at the laundry place. He figured they would be fine until he could go get them.

He returned to his room, and Dr. Reynolds looked at his hands and face.

"I'll leave the dressings off today and let your hands get some light. They should scab over well. Then, if you're careful, you can use them, and that will help the soreness go away faster."

"Thanks, Doc. I'll be outside for a while." He went

over to the wall where his guns were hanging on a peg and put on the shoulder holster and gun.

"Does that rig make your ribs hurt?" asked the doctor.

"No, not yet, anyway. I don't feel safe without some kind of weapon after the beating I got," said Canyon as he turned to go out back.

"Lucy has you a chair beside the back door. I'd appreciate it if you'd stay in the chair and not walk away."

"Okay, I'll stay close by." Canyon picked up the last biscuit and a piece of bacon left from his breakfast and went outside. A big black stray dog walked down the alley and trotted up to him and sat on its butt, looking at the biscuit in Canyon's hand. Canyon looked into the dog's eyes and for a split second, he felt a connection with the mutt. He reached out and handed the dog his biscuit. It was gone in one bite. The dog lay beside the chair, and Canyon stuck out one of his injured hands and rubbed behind the dog's ears.

The dog lifted his head and licked the scabs on the back of Canyon's right hand. At first, Canyon pulled his hand away but then put it back down and let the animal lick it. The dog stayed beside Canyon's chair, content to be close to his new friend. A few minutes later, two men came walking down the alley, and when they were close to where Canyon sat, the dog got to its feet and stood looking at them, the hair on its back bristling. Canyon reached out and softly talked to the dog to calm its fears as the men passed.

"Good boy. I don't know if you know those men and they did you wrong, or you were protecting me, but either way, you did well."

Canyon liked being outside, sitting and enjoying the sun shining down on him. Brenda had said she was going to return to Abilene and check on him. He wondered when that would be. Maybe things weren't going well at the ranch, and she couldn't leave, or maybe one of the others got sick or hurt. The dog stood up and put his head on Canyon's lap. Although Canyon had never had a dog or been around them very much, he could tell that the mutt wanted to be petted.

He looked at the dog closer, noticed how big his paws were, and said, "I'm going to name you Club, the ace of clubs."

Club lay back down and stayed close to the back door after Canyon went back inside. That night after Canyon had eaten his dinner, he took what was left out to the dog and also put out a pan of water close by.

Before bedtime that same night when he was talking to the doctor, he asked, "Doctor, do you think I can leave and go back to the Wotton ranch tomorrow? I'm a little worried that something has happened, and that might be why Brenda hasn't returned."

"Tomorrow will be six days since you came here. The Wotton girl did say she would be back in a few days. I'd like to leave the stitches in at least seven to ten days, but I don't see why you can't go home if you think the Wotton girl can remove them. All she has to do is snip them with scissors and pull. They should come right out."

"I'm sure she can do that. Tomorrow I'll plan on riding if nothing changes before then. Thanks, Doctor," said Canyon.

He had another dream, but this time he was facing thirteen men he didn't know. Suddenly the men parted and Chandler came forward. Canyon felt his heart beat faster and he began to tap his holster. Then he saw the hired gunman lying on the ground in a pool of blood. The dream drifted away as quickly as it had appeared.

CHAPTER TWENTY-THREE

Canyon was up at daylight getting dressed for his journey back to the Wotton ranch when Dr. Reynolds came in to say goodbye.

"You're probably going to be sore tomorrow. Riding all day will cause the bruises on your ribs and stomach to be more uncomfortable. I suggest you talk to the man at the livery stable and see if he has some horse liniment or healing salve you can use."

"What about my hands? Can I put the liniment on them?"

"I don't think that would be good. It might burn and irritate the skin. I'll give you some of the salve that I've been using under your bandages, and you can apply it three or four times daily. It's mostly a combination of different herbs."

"Thanks, Doctor, for all that you have done. Tell me how much I owe you, and we'll settle up so I can be on my way," said Canyon as he opened up his travel bag where his money was hidden.

"You owe me thirty-six dollars."

Canyon paid him the money. "I'm in your debt. If I

can ever help, you let me know," he said, hoping a smile would do instead of trying to shake hands.

Canyon had tied a string to his clothing satchel so he could place it over his shoulder and not have to hold it in his hands, but he needed help with getting it situated. "Doctor, would you help me with this thing?"

"Of course." Dr. Reynolds picked up the bag and placed the string over Canyon's head and one of his shoulders so that the bag dropped down by his side.

"Thanks again. I'll stop by and see you sometime when I'm in town." Canyon went out the front door.

Under his vest he had on his shoulder holster and gun, and on his right hip was his other gun. Since his hands were still sore and stiff, he probably wouldn't be able to use the weapons very effectively.

He was almost to the livery stable to get his horse when the black dog trotted up and walked beside him the rest of the way. "Boy, are you going with me, or did you come by to see me off?" The dog wagged its tail and continued to follow.

While the hustler was getting his horse saddled and ready to travel, Canyon walked to the café and bought some biscuits and fried ham for the road. The dog was lying outside the stable door waiting for him when he returned to get his horse. He gave Club one of the biscuits and said, "That will have to do for now. If you want to tag along, I'll give you another one later."

Canyon rode down the dusty street with the black dog alongside his horse and they stopped at the mercantile, where Canyon tied his horse to the hitch rail. The dog stood looking at its new friend as he dismounted.

"Stay out here," Canyon told Club.

He went into the store, where tables and shelves were stacked with various goods. They had everything from clothes, food, and guns to shovels and other equipment.

"Howdy, what can I get you today, friend?" asked the man behind the counter.

"I'd like to buy a rifle, a saddle scabbard, ammo, and jerky," said Canyon.

"I have a couple of Henry repeating rifles. You can look at them while I sack you some fresh jerky."

The store clerk went through a door behind the counter and returned with two rifles. Canyon picked one up and put it to his shoulder before looking down its barrel. The lever action was smooth, and the gun felt well balanced in his hands.

"I'll take this one."

"Good, you made a fine choice. I'll get the scabbard and ammunition for you," said the clerk. "Could I interest you in some cookware or maybe a hunting knife?"

"No, this is all I need. But if you don't mind, would you load the rifle for me? My hands are injured, and it's hard to use them."

"I normally don't do that, but I'll make an exception this time."

When the clerk had the gun fully loaded and lying on the counter, Canyon said, "Thanks a lot. Figure up my bill, and I'll be on my way."

Canyon paid for his things and went outside to find the black dog still where he had left him. It took him a few minutes to get the scabbard tied to the saddle and the ammo secured inside his saddle bags. When he got ready to mount, he tossed the dog a piece of the jerky. It was consumed in one bite.

He rode to the laundry place where he had left his clothes the day he was beaten. The Asian lady remembered him and gave him his things, clean, pressed, and tied with twine.

They were hardly out of town when he thought about

Brenda again. He'd been sure that she would come to see him. Maybe he would meet her on the road somewhere.

The gambler was at it again. He had taken a chance on a stray dog, and now he had a new friend that was leaving town with him. It was too bad the dog couldn't talk, but he seemed smart enough to learn commands and that was something Canyon would have to teach him. Canyon was glad to have a companion with him so he could talk to it and not worry about it talking back.

Switching the reins from hand to hand allowed him to keep wiggling his fingers so he could work out the soreness in his injured hands. He bought the rifle because he feared he wouldn't be strong enough to use a pistol until he healed more. The rifle would give him another option for survival if trouble came his way.

By noon, he was tired, and his side hurt from the jarring pace of his horse. He had to find a place to stop so he could get out of the heat and rest. There weren't any streams within sight, so he looked for a tree where they could sleep in the shade for a while. He spotted a scattering of cottonwood trees and figured a spring might be nearby. When he got to the trees, the ground was damp, but there was no water. He tied his horse in the shade where he could eat grass. Canyon found a stick and used it to carve out a hole in the wet ground, hoping it would fill with water.

Sure enough, the hole filled sufficiently for the dog to get a drink. After that, Canyon and the dog shared a biscuit and a slice of ham, then lay down on the grass and went to sleep.

The dog's growling woke him up, and out of habit Canyon reached inside his vest for the shoulder gun. He lifted his head and saw someone riding down the road toward Abilene. "Easy, big boy, he's just riding by," said Canyon, rubbing the dog behind its ears. "I need to be more careful the next time we stop—I left the rifle with my horse. I'm just glad I didn't need it. Come on boy, we should probably get going or I'll never make it to the ranch today."

When he got up from the hard ground, his entire body was stiff and sore. It took him a few minutes of moving around in different ways to get his muscles loosened up enough to get back on his horse.

CHAPTER TWENTY-FOUR

C anyon tried to lope his horse to make up some time that he had lost while resting, but the movement hurt his side too much, and he finally slowed to a walk. That was better for Club, anyway. The dog's tongue was hanging out of his mouth in an effort to cool off.

He could see a cloud of dust off on the horizon, like riders were coming his way. With that much dust in the air, it had to be at least six or more horses. But he could be wrong since the heat waves dancing across the range made things less clear.

He pulled the rifle from its holster and rested it across the front of his saddle. It was decision time. Did he stay on the road or veer off and find a location from which he could defend himself? The riders could be friendly, but there was no way to know for sure. And with his hands in such bad shape, he wouldn't be able to put up much of a fight. On the other hand, he had never been one to run from a fight, so he decided to stay on the road and see what would happen.

He kept his eyes on the dust rising into the sky. The

heat waves danced off the road, creating an illusion of steam rising from a pot of boiling water.

The hair on Club's back started to bristle, and the dog looked up at its new friend. Even it knew something was about to happen.

The first thing Canyon could see clearly through the rising dust was a team of horses coming toward him, and a rider on a horse alongside the fast-moving wagon. The horses were lathered up like they had been working hard.

It was Brenda on the wagon seat and Isaiah on his horse, coming as fast as the tired animals would go.

Canyon started waving his hand in the air to get them to stop. He saw Brenda pull back on the reins, and Isaiah urged his horse forward and grabbed one of the horse's bridles to help his sister stop the wagon. Then Brenda stood and climbed over the seat into the wagon bed. Canyon and his dog rode forward to meet them.

As he got closer, Canyon saw Bart lying on hay in the bed of the wagon. He was covered with a quilt, and he looked to be in bad shape. His face was bruised, lips drawn into a tight grimace. Cuts and abrasions covered his cheeks and forehead. Brenda held a canteen to her grandpa's lips to give him a drink.

"What happened to Bart?" asked Canyon.

"He went to check on the dam we built and didn't come home, so I started looking for him at the new tank we built. I found him halfway in the water, barely alive. They beat him so badly that he was almost dead by the time we got him home last night," said Isaiah.

Brenda stood up and put the cork back in the canteen. "We're on our way to the doctor. Canyon, you were right, but he wouldn't listen and had to go off alone. We need to get going. I'm afraid he won't last long out here in this heat."

"Y'all get going. I'll ride on to the ranch. Gaines's men

will try something if they know you've left. I'll protect it with my life, and if they try to take me, I'll take a few of them with me when they do. There was no need to beat an old man."

"Okay, we have to go. Be careful out there by yourself," said Brenda, slapping the reins to the horses' rumps.

A new feeling came over Canyon that he wasn't used to. It was hatred and love at the same time. He wanted to lash out at the men who beat Bart, but he also wanted to hold Brenda and keep her safe and comforted.

Now he had to ignore the pain in his body and get to the ranch as quick as possible.

Bent over in the saddle from the ache in his side, he loped his horse all the way to the ranch. It might not have been the best decision he'd ever made, but he needed to get there before the Gaines men did any more damage.

He turned off the main road and onto the lane that led to the ranch house. It was time to slow down and be watchful, in case someone was observing the house and the lane. The tops of the roofs were in sight, but he was still a half mile away when he saw two riders coming from the east toward the buildings.

Canyon put the reins in his left hand, then draped his right hand on the rifle. He couldn't grasp the gun well, but it would have to be good enough. He turned his horse toward the two riders and watched them point at him. They veered his way so they would meet up.

Canyon took his hand off the rifle and left it in its scabbard, pulled the gun from his holster, and cocked the hammer back. The pistol was much more comfortable and he had way more experience using it. He was ready for trouble, and he had no problem giving it today.

He stopped his horse and waited for the riders to come to him. When they were within thirty feet of him, he said, "That's far enough. What're you doing on the Wotton range?"

The black dog hunkered close to the ground and started to circle behind the men.

One of the riders, a man of about thirty, put one hand on his saddle horn and the other on his right leg, close to his gun. He grinned and said, "It's none of your business where we go or what we do. And say, that scar on your face looks mighty familiar."

This last remark ignited a fuse in Canyon. He brought the gun up and fired two times, hitting the man in the chest. The man tumbled off the rear of his horse and hit the ground with a thump. The dog ran toward the fallen man as if ready to attack, but stopped when he realized the man was dead.

Canyon turned the gun on the other man. "Does my scar look familiar to you also?"

The rider threw up his hands. "Mister, I was in the saloon when they beat you up and wasn't part of it. Jack and Woody were with Chandler that day. They came back into the bar and bragged about putting a gunfighter out of commission by busting up his hands."

The black dog hunched down, sneaking up behind the man's horse.

"Club, come back here and lie down," Canyon said to the dog, who did what he was told.

"This is where you choose whether you live or die. Who beat the old man down by the tank yesterday?" asked Canyon as he cocked the hammer back on his gun.

"It was Jack and Woody. They had orders to bust the dam, and I reckon the old man came upon them there, and they beat him."

"What's your name?" asked Canyon.

"It's Cooper Walls."

"By what you told me, I'm assuming that dead man is Jack, is that right?"

"Yup, that's Jack."

"What does Woody look like?"

"He's short, about five foot eight, and heavy. He has a black mole on his forehead that you can't miss."

"Load Jack onto his horse and take him with you. You give Chandler a message for me when you see him. Tell him that I'm coming for him and Woody."

"Mister, I don't know your name," said Cooper.

"It's Canyon. The man Chandler was too scared to face man-to-man, so he had to have Jack and Woody jump me from behind."

"Are you going to help me load Jack onto his horse?" asked Cooper.

"No, that's your job. Take that gun belt off and hang it on your saddle. Then you can tie a rope around Jack and drag him back to Gaines for all I care. Speaking of Gaines, give him a message from me as well. You tell him that from now on, I'll kill any man I find on the Wotton range."

"You know he ain't going to like that at all, don't you? Mr. Gaines wants all the land in these parts," said Cooper as he gripped Jack under his armpits and lifted him with all his might.

Canyon sat on his horse and watched as the man struggled to get the corpse onto the saddle.

When Cooper finally succeeded, he sat on the ground and looked up at Canyon. "I'll deliver your messages, and then I'm dragging up. I didn't sign on for a range war."

"Just one more question. Who is the little man who smokes and stays to himself?"

"That would be Weasel. You watch your back around

him. He's rumored to bushwhack people who get in his way, and it don't matter if it's man, woman, or child."

"Thanks. Now get Jack tied on to his horse and get going. I have things to do besides sitting here jawing with you."

Cooper tied the body to the saddle and headed out toward the Gaines Ranch.

Canyon waited until he was out of eyesight and rode to the house. What with everything that had happened today, he figured there would be company coming his way tomorrow and he needed to be ready.

CHAPTER TWENTY-FIVE

C anyon didn't stop at the house, instead he rode to the barn where he removed his travel bag, rifle scabbard, and the saddle before feeding his horse in one of the stalls. The gambler was so tired and sore from the ride that he could hardly walk. When he hung up the bridle in the tack room, he saw a jar of salve that Bart must have used on the animals. It smelled like herbs. After removing his shirt, he rubbed some of it on his bruises. He even put some on his palms, but left it off the backs of his hands where they were injured the worst, thinking it might inflame the skin where the scabs had already formed.

Canyon could hardly walk the distance from the barn to the house. Club walked beside him and when they got into the house, Club lay down close to the back door. Canyon went inside the kitchen and found some scraps for the dog. Then he went directly to one of the bedrooms where it was hot and stuffy, and went to sleep. He woke up sometime after midnight hot, sweating, and thirsty. He took his pistol with him to the kitchen and gulped down two dippers of warm water that was in the drinking bucket.

It was so hot inside the house that he picked up his pistol and sat outside in the dark. He figured it must be around three in the morning. The night air felt so sticky that he thought a storm might develop later that afternoon when it became sweltering and humid.

Club came to him and sat down on his hind end, rubbing his head against Canyon's leg. "Do you sense a storm coming, boy?" The dog looked at him and wagged his tail.

"We can't do anything about the weather, but if it does start to storm, you can go to the barn," he said to his hairy friend. He stayed outside for another twenty minutes before he got up. "I'm going back to bed. I suggest you do the same."

Club trotted off toward the barn, doing as he was told.

Once back in the house, Canyon decided to go ahead and get the cook stove fired up and have coffee. Since there wasn't anyone around but him and the dog, he could take a cool bath outside. The washtub hung from a nail on the back porch, and there was lye soap in the kitchen by the wash pan. Canyon took the tub, set it close to the well, and drew a bucket of water before returning to the kitchen. The stove was hot when he came in, so he made some coffee. He went back to the well and filled the tub with water, then got himself a cup and clean clothes. The cool water felt good to his bruised and sore body as he soaked and drank coffee.

It was beginning to lighten up with the sun peeking up in the east when he got out of the tub. He put on his clothes and hand-washed his dirty ones in the bathwater before hanging them on the clothesline.

After a hearty breakfast, he cleaned up the kitchen, put the washtub up, and sat on the porch drinking the last cup of coffee. It was then that he saw a wagon pulled by the biggest horse he had ever seen coming toward the house.

The wagon most likely wasn't a threat to him, so he told the dog to stay on the porch when it pulled up. "Howdy, what can I do for you?" asked Canyon.

"Is Bartholomew here? I'm Titus McBroom. My place joins Bart's on the west. I borrowed a bull from him and brought it back this morning and left it with the herd."

"I'm Canyon. I work for Bart, and he's in Abilene at the doctor's office. He got beaten badly, so Brenda took him to Dr. Reynolds."

"Gaines's men do the beating?" asked Titus.

"Yep, two men by the names of Jack and Woody."

"Those two are mean and get their kicks from hurting folks. I best be getting home. Who knows, I may be next. I'll be praying for Bartholomew."

"Nice meeting you, Titus. If it's any consolation, Jack won't be hurting anyone ever again. I met him yesterday, and he's six feet under by now."

"Well, that's good to know. But you watch out. There are still plenty of others with that outfit who are just as bad."

"Yes, sir. You take care," said Canyon as the man turned the wagon around and returned in the direction he came.

Canyon felt much better than he had the day before, so he went to the barn and saddled his horse. He wanted to go look at the tank and see what damage Gaines's men had done to it. Riding with the rifle in front of him was a little awkward, but he wanted it handy in case of trouble.

He was getting close to the tank when he turned east and rode to the top of a hill to see the valley where the creek ran through the range. The range was covered with cattle within a half mile of the tank. He knew at once that they weren't Bart's cattle by the size of the herd, and Bart didn't have that many. Gaines must have ordered his cowboys to drive his cattle onto Bart's range so they would eat all of Bart's grass, leaving none for his own cattle.

Canyon started off the hill toward the tank dam when he saw something on the ground...the butt of a cigarette. Weasel had been here snooping around. He looked the area over but didn't see any place that would make for an ambush location where the little man could hide.

The tank dam was still in good shape. Bart must have ridden up just as the men had started destroying it. What could he do about those cows east of here? He had heard that cattle could be made to stampede by shooting a gun close to them, so he thought he would have fun and try that.

When he had ridden close to the herd, he pulled his gun from the shoulder holster, fired into the air, and hollered at the top of his lungs. The dog barked and nipped at the cows' hind legs. Canyon rode his horse as close to them as he could, hollering and shooting. The cattle began to run toward the southeast along the creek bottom. When he had emptied both guns, he reloaded and kept after the cows until they had run back to their own range.

He followed them for over five miles until he figured it was time to turn back in case someone had heard the shooting and came to investigate.

About two miles from the tank, he noticed a timber stand on a hill to his right. That would be a good observation point to see if anyone was on the range heading his way.

When he entered the thick of the trees, he noticed that he wasn't the only one who had been there. Four cigarette butts lay on the ground; someone had used their boot to stomp them out. Weasel had been snooping around looking for someone, and, most likely, that would be Canyon.

Weasel was easy to follow after he left the trees. He had ridden by the tank and on toward the Wotton's house. It took some searching, but Canyon finally found a gulley about one hundred yards southwest of the house and barn. He found plenty of evidence that the evil-looking man had been lurking there, smoking and watching the house.

"Come here, Club. You look this area over and take a smell of these butts. Then it's your job to watch for this feller." Canyon smiled, knowing that the dog didn't understand one word that he said, but then again, he was an intelligent mutt.

"Come on, dog, let's go home. We've had our fun for the day, and I'm hungry."

CHAPTER TWENTY-SIX

C anyon stayed close to the house and barn the following day and kept watch toward the gully for Weasel. He hoped the dog would alert him if the man came close to the house.

His hands were getting better each day, but it would still be a few more days before he could use a shovel or swing an axe for kindling. Hopefully, the Wottons would return soon and bring good news about Bart's condition. Even though the old man was in his seventies, he had a strong mind, and hard work had kept his body in good shape. He might actually recover well, despite the ill use his body had taken.

By noon Canyon felt bored and antsy to be doing something. He had cleaned the kitchen and swept the entire house. It was time to investigate some more, so he picked up his rifle and went out the front door, and the dog followed.

They walked past the gully Weasel had been using and continued until Canyon found an impression in the ground. He lay in the hollow and waited to see if Weasel came back to his hiding spot. The dog lay beside him, and every so often would lift his head and sniff the air.

Two hours later, the sun had finally affected both man and animal. They got up and then returned to the house for water and shade.

Canyon still wanted to watch for Weasel but needed to find a better place to spy on the man. He approached the gulch and looked back toward the house and barn. An idea floated through his mind, and he started back that way.

Inside the barn, he found several short boards, nails, a hammer, and a saw. It was difficult to get the items up the ladder to the hay loft, but with some effort he managed it in decent time. If he peered through the cracks between the boards of the barn's wall, he had a clear view of the area that led into the gully.

He sawed out a couple of siding planks, then nailed up the board he'd brought with him to make a small door that could be removed. Most likely, Weasel would never see the opening as he approached the house, so it was a safe place to be. Canyon could open up the loft doors on each end of the barn so a breeze would come through, and he could keep watch in the shade.

That evening after he had eaten and fed Club, he was at the well filling up the water buckets for the kitchen when he heard the dog growl as it looked toward the house.

Canyon put the bucket down and picked up the rifle, and that was when he heard the rattle of chains and harnesses of a wagon approaching.

"Come on, Club, let's see who's coming."

He went around the east side of the house, stood by the porch post, and saw Brenda herding the team toward home at a slower pace than she had taken going to

Abilene. Isaiah rode alongside the wagon, and he and Brenda looked tired and distraught.

Canyon waited by the porch until Brenda parked the wagon nearby. He went to the front wheel and reached up to help her down. She fell into his arms, weeping and sobbing. He didn't know what to do or say, so he simply held on to her and let her cry. This was the first time a woman had ever sought genuine comfort from him. He had had his association with bar girls, but this was different in so many ways. He actually felt an emotional and physical attachment that he had never felt before for any woman. She eventually turned him loose when Isaiah said, "Come on, we should get Grandpa in the house. He's in bad shape and mighty tired."

Canyon looked in the wagon bed at the old man, who lay with his eyes closed and his chest hardly moving.

"Why did you bring him back here in such bad shape?" asked Canyon. "He should be at the doctor's place healing up."

"Grandpa wanted to come home to die," said Isaiah.

"Okay, I understand," said Canyon. "Brenda, go in the house and get a heavy quilt. We'll roll him onto it and carry him to his bed so we don't hurt him."

The three of them managed to get Bart in bed, and Brenda gave him a few swallows of water before he went unconscious.

"Y'all sit down, and I'll fix you some supper. Then you can tell me what's happened," said Canyon.

"Just heat up the coffee. I don't want anything to eat right now," said Isaiah.

"It's still hot from supper," said Canyon, taking down three cups and filling them. He put the cups on the table and sat down, waiting on either Brenda or Isaiah to start talking.

Brenda took a sip and started to cry. Canyon took one

of her hands in his. "Go ahead and let it out. Me and Isaiah are here for you."

"The doctor said that Grandpa's injuries were so bad that he couldn't do anything for him. Grandpa wanted to come home to die and be buried with Grandma and our pa," said Isaiah with tears running down his face.

Brenda clasped Canyon's hand tightly and looked him in the eyes. Something about her face had changed. Now it showed rage, hate, and trauma. "If it's the last thing I ever do, I want that whole Gaines bunch dead." She squeezed his hand harder, hurting Canyon's injuries, but he didn't let on.

"Do you hear me?" said Brenda. "I want you to teach me how to shoot a gun. They have caused my family enough grief, and I refuse to turn the other cheek anymore."

"I hear you loud and clear, but for now we have to take care of your grandpa and make him as comfortable as possible," said Canyon. "There'll be time for revenge in a few days. If it's any consolation, one of the men who beat him is dead. I killed him the day I came back. I also know who the other one is, and I'll kill him soon."

Canyon finally talked Brenda and Isaiah into going to bed with the promise that he would sit with Bart and that if anything about his condition changed, he would wake them.

Sometime before morning, Bart started to mumble, and his eyes opened and closed several times. Canyon woke up Brenda and Isaiah because he thought Bart's time was up, and perhaps the man was seeing a vision of his journey home to be with his loved ones.

They had been at his bedside only a few minutes when he again opened his eyes and reached out for Brenda and Isaiah to hold his hands. He squeezed their hands and breathed his last breath.

Brenda leaned over, kissed his cheek, and then got up and went to Canyon. "Thank you for coming and waking us up. How did you know he was about to go?"

Canyon fought back tears and paused before he said anything. "He saw Jesus coming for him."

Brenda put her arms around his neck, and he held her. "Sweetie, we need to get busy," said Canyon. "Me and Isaiah will start digging a grave if you get his favorite quilt to put him in."

"No, I want Isaiah to build him a coffin, and I'll help you dig the grave," said Brenda.

CHAPTER TWENTY-SEVEN

B renda and Canyon worked without stopping until they'd finished digging the grave early in the afternoon. They checked on Isaiah, who was putting the finishing touches on the coffin.

"Let's go harness up one of the horses and we'll put the casket in the back of the buckboard," said Brenda.

She parked the wagon in front of the house and arranged the coffin so that one end was in the wagon, and the other was on the ground. Canyon and Isaiah carried Bart outside, wrapped in a quilt, and placed him in the box. Then they slid the coffin into the wagon bed.

Canyon led the horse to the gravesite, and it took the three of them a few minutes to get the casket to the ground and lowered into the hole with ropes. Brenda grabbed a Bible she'd brought along and gave it to Canyon.

"I shouldn't be the one reading from the Bible. You or Isaiah should do it. I'm not religious, and right now I don't want to read from the Book."

"I'll do it," said Isaiah.

After he read a few verses, the three of them filled in

the grave. Isaiah had also built a wooden cross with Bart's name inscribed on it, which they erected to mark the grave.

The dog had stayed with them the entire time, lying under a shade tree. When they started back to the house, Club growled and the hair on his neck bristled. Canyon kept walking and told the dog to stay with them. When they entered the house, Canyon grabbed his rifle. "Stay away from the windows and doors. Someone is out there, and I intend to find out who it is."

"I'm going with you," said Brenda.

"No, you can't come with me," said Canyon. "If it's who I think it is, I don't want you anywhere near him. I think it's the man called Weasel, and he's very dangerous. I can't watch out for both of us. Isaiah, go get your grandpa's gun and stay put. If anyone besides me comes in the house, shoot them."

Canyon walked to the barn and climbed up to the loft where he had made his observation window. Although he had a good view of the gully, he couldn't see anyone. This was not working like he had planned. It was time to do something else. He climbed down the ladder, went to the stall where his horse was and put the saddle on it. He led the animal out of the barn and mounted up. As soon as he was in the saddle, he leaned over his horse's neck and put the spurs to him. The dog tried to keep up with them as they headed toward the gully where Canyon thought Weasel was lurking.

Before he got to the ravine, he saw Weasel come out of hiding and take off on his horse, heading back toward the Gaines's range. Canyon stayed after him, knowing that Weasel's horse was most likely tired. His own was fresh and would eventually catch up.

Canyon veered off to the east and went over a hill to shorten the distance between him and the man he was after. Unfortunately, he couldn't see the dog anywhere, and about the time Weasel skirted around the tank, the dog came at his horse with teeth bared, causing the beast to rear up. By the time Weasel had his horse under control, Canyon was coming up fast. He slammed his horse into the little man's scared mount and Weasel fell to the ground onto his back.

Canyon jumped from the back of his horse and dropped the rifle, and the gun on his hip slid out of the holster by accident and hit the ground. The two men got to their feet at about the same time, and Canyon noticed Weasel had a long blade knife in his hand. The man hunched down like he was going to charge waving the blade back and forth in front of himself.

Club was in a crouch getting into position for his second attempt at the evil man. "Club, stay put," said Canyon. "I'm going to kill this bushwhacker and send him to hell."

The little evil man swiped his knife at Canyon. "That's mighty big talk for a man without a weapon." He laughed and pointed at the hip gun, which lay several feet away.

A look of shock crossed Canyon's face. He brought his left hand to his mouth and his eyes went wide, as if he was scared. And just like that, his right hand pulled the gun from his shoulder holster and fired one shot that entered the man's left eye and exploded out the back of his skull.

When Weasel hit the ground, the dog ran up and bit a chunk out of his throat just to make sure the man was dead. He didn't eat it but opened his mouth, letting the flesh hit the ground. Canyon looked on in silence at what the dog had done and surmised that it wasn't his first time in battle either.

Club trotted off and lay down while his master

removed Weasel's gun belt from his waist and pulled the rifle from the scabbard on his horse. He found three boxes of shells in the dead man's saddlebags and took them too.

Canyon reloaded his gun and picked up his other weapons before removing a length of rope from the lifeless man's horse. He tied a rope around his legs before tying the other end to the saddle horn and slapped the horse on the rump. The horse headed home, dragging Weasel's body behind him.

Canyon and Club stood watching until the horse slowed to a walk about a half mile away. With careful aim of the rifle, he fired one shot that landed close to the horse. It reacted by running off, dragging the body behind it until they were out of sight.

"Come on, boy, let's go home and get a drink of water and a snack. You did a great thing today by stopping that horse." Canyon rubbed the dog's head. Weasel was the one man he had wanted dead. From the first time he had seen the little man, he thought he was the most dangerous and would need killing first. As he and Club went back toward the house, he knew this was all going to be all right in the end. That was what all the dreams he had been having were telling him.

He hollered out when he pulled up to the back of the house. "Don't shoot, I'm back!"

CHAPTER TWENTY-EIGHT

B renda came running out of the house and hugged Canyon's neck when he dismounted. The dog walked up to her and started to sniff her shoes. "Let him smell your hands. He's very protective, and he needs to know you're his friend. He'll guard you when I'm not around if you rub behind his ears and give him food to eat," said Canyon.

"Where on earth did you find him?" asked Brenda as she let the dog sniff her hand.

"We sort of found each other and he followed me here. We're just now really getting to know each other, but you'll soon learn that he's smarter than some people."

Once Club accepted her, he rubbed his head against her leg and she scratched him behind his ears for a few seconds. "I swear, he needs a bath in the worst way. This dog stinks to high heaven."

Canyon laughed. "Don't insult him! He's a sensitive animal. Come on, let's give him a snack. He deserves it after what he did today."

"We heard a shot. I'm assuming you killed that

terrible man," said Brenda as she went through the back door.

"Yeah, he's dead and on his way back to Gaines's ranch. What's left of him, that is."

"What do you mean?"

"I tied him to his horse and pointed it toward the ranch," said Canyon, leaving out the part about Weasel being dragged back.

He sat down at the table while Brenda gathered a couple of hard biscuits for the dog. When she had thrown them out to him, she asked, "What is your dog's name?"

"He's our dog now, and his name is Club. He's got the biggest paws and he's black, like the ace of clubs."

Brenda brushed a strand of hair from her face. "I see, so our dog is going to be a gambler like you?"

Canyon smiled at her. "I'd like to talk to you and Isaiah about another matter. Would you go get him while I get something from my horse?" said Canyon.

"Sure," said Brenda.

Canyon left the house and returned carrying the guns and ammunition he had taken off Weasel. He put everything on the table.

"This gun belt is too small for Isaiah, so you can have it, Brenda. Try it on and see if it'll fit."

She put it on and he adjusted it so the gun would be easy for her to draw. Then he handed the repeating rifle to Isaiah. "This rifle will most likely shoot fourteen or fifteen rounds. Let's go outside and start your training on how to use your new toys."

As soon as they stepped into the backyard, Club came to Isaiah and sniffed his hand. Isaiah leaned over and petted the dog, who began to wag his tail.

"Come on, you two. We have work to do before dark."

Canyon showed them how to operate their guns and

made them load and unload the weapons multiple times. Next, he made Brenda stand with her feet shoulder-width apart and practice drawing the pistol without aiming it. She just pulled and pointed. He made Isaiah put the rifle to his shoulder as fast as he could and practice working the lever.

When Canyon felt confident about how they handled the guns, he had them load up their weapons. "Brenda, you'll go first. I want you to focus on where you're going to shoot. Pull the pistol from the holster, pull the hammer back, and fire as you're extending your arm toward your target."

She did as he instructed, but the first two shots fell short of their mark. She readjusted and tried again, and after three reloads, she hit the target where she pointed the weapon.

Next it was Isaiah's turn. He quickly put the rifle to his shoulder and fired. The first bullet hit the mark, but when he worked the lever action for another shell, he missed. By the time he had shot all his rounds, he was hitting his targets consistently.

"Okay, it'll be dark soon. Let's go to the house and fix supper. We'll practice some more tomorrow."

"Canyon, Grandpa's room is now your room. We moved all his things out while you went after that bad man. Unfortunately, Grandpa is dead and never returning, so we need to move on with our lives."

"Yes, we do. I lost both my parents a few years back, and it was hard. But life is a gamble, and it does go on, and we need to make the best of it," said Canyon.

"It's hard to accept, but you're right. Life does go on," said Brenda.

"Could I get you to do something for me?" asked Canyon.

"Of course, what do you want?"

"Would you get your scissors and some pliers and remove the stitches from my cheek? The doctor said you could do it, and it's time."

"I've never done that before, but I can try. I'll go get my things and be right back."

Brenda had him sit in a kitchen chair and bring the lantern close so she could work with good light. He could hear her cut the horsehair thread, and then she started to jerk the stitches from his cheek. There was a little discomfort, but nothing he couldn't handle. When she was finished, she ran her fingertips along the scar.

"I'm sorry you have this scar. I never notice the mark on your face. I see the man that I love." She leaned down and kissed his cheek. "Let me look at your hands." She inspected them and said, "They're healing nicely, and I think you can start putting liniment on them soon."

Canyon looked at his fingers and made a fist. "Yep, they are healing, and most of the soreness is gone. I've been rubbing liniment into the palms but not the tops. I may do that in a few days. Thanks for removing my stitches. I think it's time to call it a night and get some shut-eye."

Brenda put her scissors up and hugged him before she went to her room. Canyon blew out the lights and got ready to go to sleep.

He laid in his bed that night, thinking about life and death. Life could be challenging at times, but it could also be wonderful. He felt so blessed that he had Brenda and Isaiah in his life. He had wanted a profession other than gambling, where it seemed that he always had to use his gun. All he knew how to do was play poker, sweep floors, and perform manual labor on a loading dock somewhere like his pa did. He felt that he was using his skills now for a different, better reason and purpose. By all rights, he should be dead either from the gunshot or the beating by Chandler and his men. A higher power had brought him through both of those situations, and he had seen vision or dreams. Helping someone fight against a bully was something he wouldn't back away from because he felt deep down in his heart that God had a purpose for him and would protect him.

He smiled. Why even think about death? It was the only thing in life that was guaranteed. They were all going to die sometime. Canyon knew he needed to make the most of each day, month, and year he had left.

CHAPTER TWENTY-NINE

When they finished breakfast and the chores were done the following morning, Canyon went behind the barn and set up shooting targets. This time Isaiah when first, and after six shots, Canyon had him shoot from the hip without aiming. Isaiah lifted the gun to hip level and shot where he pointed. He improved with each round, and when his gun was empty, that was enough for him. They needed to save as many bullets as they could.

Brenda continued to shoot the same as the previous day. Her gun was a little heavy for her, but she figured out how to pull the weapon and fire quicker so its weight didn't hinder her shot.

He let her shoot two chambers and then drew his own pistol as fast as he could. After six practice draws and shots to see how his hand would do under pressure, he said, "We're stopping for the day. I don't want to use up any more ammunition on target practice."

"Do you think Gaines will try something today?" asked Isaiah.

"He could, but I'm more concerned about tomorrow," said Canyon.

"Do you think the man you killed was a spy or up to something else?" asked Brenda.

"I think both. Weasel had been watching the house for a few days. I found his cigarette butts at a couple of locations. I suspect he had orders to watch the ranch, and if he got the opportunity to catch one of you alone, he would have killed you."

"Grandpa thought we were being watched for a while. He wouldn't do anything about it because he knew he was outnumbered and had no chance against Gaines."

"We might not either, but I guarantee you that we'll take some of them with us if they come calling," said Canyon. He turned to Isaiah. "It's only around ten. Can you ride to Abilene, buy us more ammo, and get back by tonight?"

"Yeah, I can probably be back sometime tonight, but I sure can get back earlier if I left out first thing in the morning."

Canyon thought for a few seconds. "Is there any place closer than Abilene that sells gun shells?"

Brenda motioned with her hand to the north. "There's a store out on the range north of here that might have ammunition. I went there with my pa a few times when we needed provisions. He liked to drink, and that was the closest place to buy a bottle of rotgut."

"I've been there with Grandpa. I can make it there and back today if I leave now," said Isaiah.

Canyon reached into his pocket and pulled out some money. "Brenda, let's go get a piece of paper to write down the caliber of bullets we need while Isaiah gets saddled and meets us at the house."

Brenda and Canyon stood on the porch and watched

Isaiah until he was out of sight. Then she put her arm around Canyon. "Now that he's gone, what are you and I going to do today?" she asked in a playful tone.

"I'm glad you asked," said Canyon. "We'll saddle up, check the tank dam, and look at the cattle. I've already run off a big herd of Gaines's cattle east of the tank while you were in Abilene. We'll have to be extra careful and keep our eyes peeled for riders. I don't know if it'll be safe out on the range after today, so you'll need to keep your gun ready all the time."

She removed her arm from around him and punched him on the shoulder. "I had other things in mind that we could do today that didn't involve the range or cattle."

He smiled and kissed her. "We have the rest of our lives together for that. Today we need to get prepared for a fight."

"You're right, my darling, and did you just propose to me?" she asked, looking up at him with her hands on her hips and her head cocked to one side.

He took her in his arms and kissed her again. "Maybe I did, but perhaps I didn't. All I can say is, you'll know without a doubt if I do."

She looked sad for a moment, but then smiled. "Just so you know, I've been in love with you since the first time I saw you."

He smiled and moved a strand of hair from in front of her face. "I know that, and I hope you know I love you too. Now we need to get going and check on things before the Gaines's men ride this way."

"Okay, I'll go get my hat. Do you want me to take us something to eat while we're out riding?"

"That'd be nice. I'll fill both of our canteens at the well. Be sure and put your hair under your hat. I want anyone who sees us to think that you're a man. That'll give them the idea that Bart has hired more help, and maybe they'll think twice about attacking the house."

"Is the dog coming with us?" asked Brenda.

"Since Isaiah is gone to the store, I think I'll make him stay here and protect the house."

"I swear, sometimes you act like that dog can understand everything you tell him," said Brenda.

Canyon whistled and Club came trotting up. Canyon rubbed behind his ears and said, "Boy, you stay here and protect the house. I'll be back later."

The dog took off to find shade, and Canyon looked at Brenda and grinned. She shook her head and went into the house to get her things.

CHAPTER THIRTY

C anyon and Brenda rode side by side when they left the house. They were armed for battle, but he hoped they wouldn't have to use their guns.

"I'd like to check on the cattle close to the south tank first," said Canyon. "They're the farthest away from Gaines's range and less likely to get harmed."

"Okay. The easiest way there is to ride west and then turn south. We never go in the direction that we're headed; it's kind of the long way and takes longer to get there."

"That's the reason I'm going this way. If anyone is watching, they'll not expect us to get there from this direction. They could be waiting for us on the usual trail."

"I never thought of it that way. So we should use different routes when we go anywhere, even to the barn?"

"That's correct. Keep your eyes open for anything that's out of place or moving. We don't want any surprises today."

After another mile, Brenda pointed toward a grass-covered hill. "There're some of our cattle over there."

"There shouldn't be cattle this close to the house. Pull your gun and be ready to shoot. I don't think those are your cattle," said Canyon as he removed his rifle from its scabbard.

"They're not ours; they have the Rocking G branded on their hips. Gaines will do anything to hurt us, even letting his cows take the grass from our cattle. Should we separate a little in case someone is with the cows and wants to start something?" asked Brenda.

Canyon nodded. "That's a good idea, but let's not get out of hearing range of each other. We'll ride through the middle of the herd. You watch to your left, and I'll tend to the right. I feel like this is a setup; whoever is here will wait until they have a good, clear shot."

The cows began to move out of the way of the horses as they rode through the herd. They were almost to the other side when Brenda said, "Canyon, I just saw a reflection off something shiny over in that clump of trees straight ahead of us."

"Turn your horse around now and go back the way we came. Someone's in there and has a rifle pointed at us. Don't look back. I don't want them to know you saw them."

When they were back at the edge of the herd where they had first entered, Canyon said, "As soon as we make it clear of the cattle, we'll turn our horses around and start hollering and firing our guns in the air. I want to start a stampede. Hopefully the cows will go through the trees where you saw the flash."

"What do I do when my gun is empty? I don't think I can reload while I'm riding," said Brenda.

Canyon handed her his shoulder holster gun. "Put

this somewhere safe and when your gun is empty, use it as your backup."

They turned their horses toward the cattle and began to holler and fire their weapons into the air. The frightened cattle started to run away from them toward the trees. Canyon continued to fire his rifle even after Brenda had emptied her pistol. She still whooped and hollered, pushing her horse to run faster. She and Canyon could feel the frightened cow's hooves pounding against the ground as dust rose into the air, obstructing their view.

Canyon put five bullets into his rifle as a few of the stampeding cattle began to run into the trees where Brenda saw the flash of light off a gun barrel. One man on horseback took off from his hidden location among the trees. He had only ridden thirty feet when Canyon shot him from the saddle.

Canyon and Brenda followed the frightened cattle and found what was left of a makeshift camp where three of Gaines's men had been staying. Two horses were staked in the grass, and one man lay dead on the ground, trampled by the stampeding cattle.

Brenda pointed up at a tree. "Look, Canyon—a human squirrel!"

Canyon pointed his rifle at the man. "Climb on down, or I'll shoot you down."

"Don't shoot! I'm unarmed, and I'll come down on my own," said the frightened cowboy.

When the man was on the ground, Canyon asked, "What's your name, and who were the other two?"

"Mister, the three of us are just hired cowboys assigned to that herd you ran off. I'm John Thompson. That feller you shot off his horse was Marty, and this one went by Tater."

"Canyon, look!" Brenda pointed to the southeast.

"That man you shot isn't dead. I just saw him try to get up."

"John, start walking over to Tater, and let's see how bad he's hurt," said Canyon.

Tater had rolled over onto his back and was holding his right shoulder. Canyon slid his rifle back into its scabbard and pulled out the pistol that was on his hip. "John, take his gun from its holster and hand it to me."

Canyon never took his eyes off John until he had Tater's gun. "You and Tater are free to go. I suggest you find another place to work because I'll kill you the next time I see you on our range. And when you return to the Gaines's headquarters, you can tell Gaines and Chandler that Canyon is coming for them."

"Mister Canyon, I can't speak for anyone but myself. You won't be seeing me again. I'm pulling my pay and leaving this war to the gun hands Gaines has on his payroll."

"I think you're making a good decision," Canyon said, holstering his gun. "Come on, Brenda, let's keep riding. We still have more places to check on."

When they had ridden a few hundred yards, Brenda asked, "What will we do with those cows we ran off?"

"I'm hoping they stopped running once they got off your range. We'll keep riding and see if they ran past the tank. If they haven't, we'll push them farther toward the Rocking G."

CHAPTER THIRTY-ONE

Gaines's cattle had run past the tank and could be seen off to the east grazing by the time Canyon and Brenda arrived to check the water level in the pond. Brenda let her horse start down to get a drink, but Canyon called out to her. "Hold up, let's check out around the hills before we get water. Someone could be waiting on us."

They rode a wide circle around the tank, and everything looked peaceful, so they went to the water's edge and let their horses drink.

Canyon looked up at the position of the sun. "I reckon we should be heading back. The sun will go down in a couple of hours, and we should be at the house when Isaiah returns."

"My brother is fifteen years old. He doesn't need us to be home when he returns. I'm not his nursemaid and sure not his ma," said Brenda.

"I'm sorry, I didn't mean it like that," said Sawyer. "I meant I want to see if Isaiah was able to buy any ammunition, or heard anything at the store about Gaines or his gun hands."

"I know. I didn't mean to snap at you," said Brenda. She rode up close enough to reach out and touch his arm.

Canyon leaned over and kissed her on the cheek. "It's okay. Let's get on home and start supper."

Club ran out to meet them with his tail wagging and barking as they rode into the yard.

"Canyon, we have to give this dog a bath. I can smell him from up here on my horse," said Brenda.

"If you get the washtub, I'll draw you a few buckets to heat while I put the horses up."

Canyon went to the back of the house to find the washtub set up in the backyard. Brenda was drawing water when he came to her and took the rope. "If you put two more buckets in there, I'll get the hot water," said Brenda.

"This could be a real pain to get him in the tub and hold him still while you bathe him," said Canyon as he started after the dog.

Brenda called out, "Come here, Club." The dog came to her and stepped into the tub and stood calmly as she wet his fur and rubbed lye soap all over him.

"I can't believe he's just standing there letting you wash him," said Canyon.

"If I was a betting woman, I would say he's been bathed a lot. He's too calm for this to be his first time."

"I agree, and for your information, he's been trained to do other things. I know for a fact that he follows commands and he knows what to do in a fight."

"What do you mean by that?" asked Brenda with a bewildered look on her face.

"As soon as I shot Weasel, Club ran up to him to make sure he was dead," said Canyon but left out the part where the dog tore a hunk from the dead man's throat.

"I'm glad he's here with us now. I know he'll let us know if someone comes sneaking around," said Brenda.

"Yes, and he'll protect us with his life," said Canyon and commenced to draw a bucket of water to rinse the soap off the dog.

When Brenda was satisfied that she had thoroughly scrubbed everywhere, Canyon rinsed him with several buckets of water. Whenever he poured a bucket on the dog, he shook his entire body and got water all over Brenda.

"He's got me soaked! I'm going to need to wash off now too," said Brenda.

"Let's get him out of the tub, and I'll bring you more water to heat up. After all this, we both could use a good soaking," said Canyon.

It was nearly dark by the time they'd both had baths and dressed in clean clothes. Brenda started supper while Canyon put the chickens in the coop for the night and fed the horses. He was walking back to the house when he saw Isaiah approaching.

"How was your trip?" asked Canyon.

Isaiah handed Canyon a flour sack. "Here're the bullets. The sack is kind of heavy."

Canyon looked inside and saw seven boxes of shells. "It looks like you did all right. Go on in the house and get washed up for supper. Take the sack with you, and I'll see after your horse."

Canyon unsaddled the horse and fed him oats, then went to the house to eat. Isaiah was already seated at the table when Canyon walked into the kitchen.

"Supper's ready, so take a seat. Today we'll hold hands and give thanks before we eat. Just because Grandpa isn't here anymore doesn't mean we stop praying," said Brenda as she set the last bowl on the table.

She sat down and reached her hands out to Isaiah and Canyon.

"Brenda, I don't pray, so it'll be up to one of you," said Canyon.

"I'll do it," said Isaiah. "Lord, thank you for this day and the food we're about to eat. Bless it to our bodies, in Jesus's name. Amen."

Canyon felt slightly embarrassed for not knowing how to pray or what to say. He didn't say anything as plates of food were passed, but he decided that he would start reading the Good Book and try to learn about God.

They ate in silence, and when Brenda pushed her plate away, she said, "Isaiah, tell us about your trip to the store."

"I made it there just fine and didn't see anyone on the way. However, three horses were tied outside the front door when I got there around noon. I waited to the south by a woodshed until they came out because I saw the Rocking G brand on their mounts. I didn't recognize any of the men, but I suspected they were cowboys since they had on chaps, and none of them wore tied-down holsters."

"Which way did they go when they left the store?" asked Canyon.

"They rode off east. There's a road that goes east and then turns southeast back toward Albany. I asked the store owner if he knew the men, and he said that they come in about once a month for tobacco and hard candy."

"I see that you bought a lot of shells," said Brenda.

"I bought all the ammo that would fit the guns we have. Unfortunately, the store didn't have a lot of shells, but the owner said he'll have more next week," said Isaiah.

"When I asked him if he's heard any rumblings over the range, he did say that there was a lot of talk going around about something big that was about to happen. The Gaines's men are on the hunt for the man that killed

Jeff Gaines. He also said that the small ranchers are scared that Gaines is getting ready to start a range war to take their land. Of course that is just rumors and speculation. No one had any proof of that."

"That's all he had to say?" asked Canyon.

"He said that Chandler stopped in on his way to Abilene. He thinks that the gunman went there to meet another gunhand," said Isaiah.

Canyon sighed. "That figures. Bring in more firepower to kill a gambler, his girlfriend, and her brother. Did he mention who he thought the new man might be?"

"No sir. I bought my things and left after that."

"Do you reckon that man at the store sells any dynamite?" asked Canyon.

"I don't know," said Isaiah. "If you need dynamite, Grandpa has a few sticks buried behind the barn under the big oak tree. He used it to remove tree stumps and such."

"Okay. Let's help Brenda clean up the kitchen, and then we can all go outside and sit in the cool of the evening," said Canyon.

Brenda washed while Canyon dried the dishes. Isaiah swept the floor and fed Club his supper. Then they each poured themselves a glass of water and went to the front porch to sit.

"Canyon, why did you ask about the dynamite?" asked Brenda when she was seated.

"We might need it in a few days to show Gaines we mean business."

Brenda told Isaiah about the herd she and Canyon had found on their land and the three men watching it. She explained how it was unsafe for him to go off alone. Canyon agreed with her.

They sat in silence for a while as Canyon petted Club. When he stopped, he said, "I took more guns off those fellers we came across today. I'm pretty sure there's a holster that'll fit you, Isaiah, and a spare gun. I still believe we'll have company at the house before this ends."

The dog left Canyon and lay down by Isaiah so he could pet him. "I saw the guns in the living room. I'll get one of the holsters when I go back in," said Isaiah.

"What are the plans for tomorrow?" asked Brenda.

"I'm not sure yet, but we better finish all our chores by nine every day. If Gaines and his men do come to the house, I don't figure on them getting here any earlier than that. We have enough guns to place some at each window and make our visitors think there are more hands here than there really are," said Canyon.

"That's a good idea," said Brenda. "We can fire and then move and fire again."

"That's right." Canyon stood up. "It's getting late. We should turn in and get some rest. In case we have company, I suggest you keep a pistol by your bed at night."

"Would it be all right if I let Club sleep in my room?" asked Isaiah.

Club stood up and looked at Brenda as if he needed her permission. She started to say something but then stopped. A few seconds later, she said, "Yes, he can sleep in your room, but it's your responsibility to care for him and sweep your floor. I don't want dog hair on everything."

"Thanks." The boy headed into the house with the dog following him.

Brenda looked at Canyon. "You might be right. I do believe that dog understands what we say."

Canyon laughed at her remark. "Come on, let's go in."

CHAPTER THIRTY-TWO

The following morning, after everyone had eaten breakfast and pitched in washing the dishes, Canyon made work assignments for Isaiah and himself.

"Isaiah, I'd like you to fill the wood box in the kitchen and then gather eggs from the chicken house."

"Do you want me to let them out in the yard while I'm at it?" asked Isaiah.

"I suppose so. Do what y'all usually do with the chickens. Once you've finished that, could you help me at the barn? I'll need your help checking the horses' shoes and cleaning all the leather with saddle soap."

"I can help with the saddle soap," said Brenda. "We usually help Grandpa with that a few times a year."

"Okay. Do you also pack the wheels on the wagon, or do you take it somewhere to get it done?"

"We do that here. Grandpa has a wagon jack in the barn so we can lift one wheel at a time," said Isaiah. "There's also tools and a bucket of grease and rags out there."

"Y'all bring your guns when you come to the barn. Club will be on the watch for anyone visiting, won't you, boy?" Canyon rubbed behind the dog's ears. He looked at Brenda. "I'll admit that he smells much better."

Everyone laughed at the remark.

Canyon, Brenda, and Isaiah were in the barn and had the saddles and bridles laid out so they could clean and treat the leather. Brenda was humming a tune when Canyon stopped and said, "Listen, that sounds like Club growling. Get your guns and keep out of sight of the front door."

Canyon picked up his rifle and walked outside. Club stood between the barn and house, looking toward the south. The hair on his back was bristling and he growled at something that Canyon couldn't see. "What's out there, boy?"

Then he saw a cloud of dust in the air. It was a mile or more away, but he knew riders were coming their way. "Everyone, run to the house, now!"

Canyon went to the barn doors and closed them as Brenda and Isaiah ran toward the house. He came behind them, running as fast as he could with Club beside him, but at the last second, the dog left his side and took off behind the house.

Once everyone was inside, Canyon gave more assignments. "Isaiah, you put one of the rifles on that left side of the window and fix it to look like someone is holding it with the barrel exposed to the riders. Then you put the other one on the right side, and that's where you'll take aim, but you be sure to keep yourself hidden so they can't shoot you. If we start shooting, you fire a couple of shells with your rifle and then crawl under the window to the other gun and fire."

"Yes sir, I can do that," said the boy, placing his guns as he was told. Brenda did the same on the window east of the door.

"Do you think it's Gaines himself or some of his men?" asked Brenda.

When Canyon was about to answer her, they heard a loud explosion and felt the ground shake. Canyon shook his head. "I reckon they just blew up our little dam across the creek."

"Where's the dog?" asked Isaiah. "I don't want him getting hurt."

"He's most likely around at the back of the house. That's a smart animal, and he knows we can't protect the front and back at the same time," said Canyon. "Don't worry about Club. He can take care of himself, and if someone does come around to the back, may God have mercy on him if that dog decides to attack."

"I'm going to get us each a glass of water," said Brenda. "This waiting makes me thirsty."

Canyon nodded and pulled the gun from his shoulder holster to check that it was fully loaded.

Brenda returned with three glasses of water and handed one to each man. "Canyon, there are still two pistols on the kitchen table. Do you want me to bring them in here in case we need them?" she asked.

"Please do, and bring in extra ammunition if you can carry it."

The pounding of horse hooves hitting the hard ground thundered up the lane, and eight riders pulled up about forty feet in front of the house.

Canyon eased the door open a few inches. "Howdy, what do you want?"

A large man wearing an orange-and-white checkered shirt and a sizable western-style hat with a wide brim sat on his palomino horse in front of the other riders. His gray facial hair and wrinkles around his eyes made him look old.

"I'm Paul Gaines, and you're squatting on my range.

You better be gone by noon tomorrow, or we'll bury you here."

Canyon stepped out the door with his right hand by the gun on his hip, his index finger tapping on the holster. "That's mighty big talk from a man that's about to die. Your hired killer, Weasel, wasn't successful in killing me. Your hired gun Chandler and his cronies couldn't put me down, and you sure won't either. I know what you did to our tank dam, and it hurts my feelings. So here's the way that this can play out. You and me can square off right here in the yard and I'll kill you and most likely two or three of your men. My associates in the house have their rifles aimed at y'all and will kill another three of four. But none of that will matter because you'll be the first to die."

Gaines pulled back on the reins of his horse and made him back up. "You've been warned and have until tomorrow at noon. Come on men, let's go." He turned his horse and they all took off.

Canyon stood in the yard watching them ride back toward the Rocking G Ranch. When the riders were out of sight, he went back into the house.

"Isaiah, show me where that dynamite is buried. I think it's the perfect time to blow up Gaines's dam on his lake, don't you?"

The boy looked at Canyon and smiled from ear to ear. "I sure do."

They went outside and Isaiah dug up a wooden box wrapped in a tarpaulin. Ten dynamite sticks lay inside the box.

"Where're the fuses?" asked Canyon.

"They're in the barn," said Isaiah. "I'll go get them."

"Get a couple of post-hole diggers also. We'll need to dig holes in the embankment," said Canyon. "Do either one of you know how to set off the dynamite? I ain't never even seen any, let alone used it."

Brenda nodded. "Isaiah knows how to do it. He went with Grandpa whenever they needed to blast something."

"We need to take a packhorse. Let's secure the box and post-hole diggers on the pony. The dynamite should ride just fine—when I opened the box, I didn't see any sweat on the sticks," said Isaiah.

"What are you talking about?" asked Canyon.

"Grandpa said that if you keep it cool and dry, it won't sweat. But it can get volatile if the stuff inside starts leaking out," said Isaiah.

"So based on what you saw, the box is safe to ride on the pack saddle?" asked Canyon.

"Yep, let's get it tied on and head out," said Isaiah. "It's a good way to the lake dam and we probably shouldn't run the horses while we're carrying this cargo."

Canyon, Brenda, Isaiah, and Club headed toward the lake dam.

CHAPTER THIRTY-THREE

Brenda looked pretty that afternoon, her hair blowing in the wind as her hat bounced on the back of her neck by the chin strap. Canyon couldn't help but look at her and see the strong lines of determination in her face. Her hazel eyes had a particular reflection today as the three rode with the sun to their backs.

"Canyon, won't they have guards at the lake dam to protect it?" asked Brenda.

He smiled mischievously at her. "Darling, I'm a gambler, and today both sides bluffed. Gaines tried to scare us away, then threatened to kill us. He's the big man in these parts of the range and doesn't feel threatened by anyone. He thinks that everyone is afraid of him and his men. So to answer your question, no, he won't have any guards on his dam, but I wouldn't be surprised if he has three or four men watching our blown-up dam."

"But why would he do that?" asked Brenda.

"He's predictable. The men who blew the dam weren't with him at the house. They were still at the dam to see if we would ride there and survey the damage. That's why we're riding wide of the tank and going

166

straight to his lake. When we blow the dam at his reservoir, the water will come rushing down the creek and over its banks. I'm betting that the men who are waiting for us will hear the explosion and come here to check out the blast. We'll be waiting on them, and that will eliminate some more of his hired guns."

"So you are gambling on how this will pan out today?" asked Brenda.

"I don't think it's a gamble. I look at it as a pat hand." Canyon smiled with confidence.

They rode silently for another two miles until Canyon took the lead and motioned for them to follow him. "We're not far from the lake, so let's ride through the creek bottom the rest of the way. When the water breaks free, it will wash away our tracks."

"It looks like a lot of horses have been coming this way," said Isaiah.

"Yep, I suspect this is how they get to us. We may want to hole up on those hills on either side of us to waylay them when they come after us," said Canyon.

When he could see the massive embankment of dirt that held back the water in the lake, Canyon raised his hand for the others to stop. "I'll ride on in and make sure we don't have a greeting party waiting on us. You two stay here until I signal."

Canyon removed the rifle from its scabbard and trotted his horse to the dam. He didn't see anyone, so he waved his hat, then rode back down to the foot of the dam where he assumed they would place the charges and waited for the others to join him.

When Isaiah, Brenda, and the packhorse had caught up, Canyon looked at Isaiah and said, "I think we should start digging holes here. How far apart do you think will be enough to blow a hole in the soil?"

"We should go up the slope a little farther and dig

holes about six feet apart toward the top. I think we'll have enough charges to take out the middle of the embankment," said Isaiah.

Isaiah and Canyon went to work with the post-hole diggers, and it didn't take them long before they had enough holes for Isaiah to start putting in the fuses and plugging a stick of dynamite into each hole. When Canyon had finished his work, he tied both of the diggers to the packsaddle.

Isaiah had the two rolls of charges tied together so that he could light both sets of fuses from about fifty yards away. Canyon and Brenda mounted up, and Canyon had the lead rope of the pack animal. "Brenda, let's me and you start riding away. Isaiah can light the fuses and catch up."

Canyon and Brenda had made it to the top of the next hill below the dam when Isaiah lit the fuses and hightailed it out of there. All three ran their horses as fast as they could and thirty seconds later, the charges began to go off. There was a constant rumble of explosions until all ten of the sticks of dynamite had exploded. The ground shook, and smoke and dust rose into the sky.

Canyon looked back at the dam, but no water was flowing through the vast void the explosion had caused. He was about to investigate when the water suddenly burst through and crashed into the creek bed.

"It looks like the charges did their job," said Brenda.

"Yeah, they did," replied Canyon. "Now let's get to that narrow valley up ahead and see if company comes our way."

They rode as fast as possible. Canyon had to keep pulling on the packhorse's lead rope until Brenda got behind the animal and whacked it with her bridle reins every time it tried to slow down. They had entered into the narrow valley with the creek running through it when they were approached by four riders coming their way.

"Riders up ahead," said Isaiah.

Canyon dropped the lead rope and pulled his shoulder pistol and the gun on his hip. The men were coming straight at them. Brenda and Isaiah pulled their guns, ready for battle.

"Hold your fire until I shoot," said Canyon. He put the bridle reins in his mouth so he could shoot with both guns.

He waited until the men were closer, then raised both guns and began to fire at the four men who immediately began to fire back.

Canyon and his small group rode past the men, then turned around to shoot some more, but all four men lay dead on the ground.

"Is anyone hurt?" asked Canyon as he reloaded his pistols.

"I'm fine," said Brenda and did like her boyfriend and reloaded her gun.

"That's four that won't be coming for us again," said Isaiah.

"I'd like the two of you to return to the house. I'll scout around and make sure none of Gaines's men come after us tonight. Club can come with me. He may be of great service in the dark; he can see better than me."

"I wish you would come home with us," said Brenda.

"I'll be along directly. But first I want to see who comes to inspect the dam," said Canyon.

"Okay, but be careful and don't get caught," said Brenda. "Come on, Isaiah, let's go home."

Canyon turned back to the broken dam and watched the water go down the creek with great force. Since he couldn't get to the other side, he rode along the lake's edge until the large body of water began to narrow. He found a hill covered with cedar trees where he could hide and wait. A short time later, he saw two riders on the other side of the lake running their mounts toward the destroyed embankment. One of the men was a short, heavy man, and he figured that it must be Woody.

Canyon went toward the upper end of the lake, then crossed over and rode toward the two men. When he came upon them, they had their backs to him, standing and watching the earthen dam continue to erode.

"Hello Woody," hollered Canyon. The short, heavy man turned in time to be met by a bullet to the head. The other man with Woody went for his gun but was too slow. Two more shots and the man was hit in his chest.

Canyon rode on past the bodies and headed home to be with Brenda and Isaiah.

CHAPTER THIRTY-FOUR

B renda and Isaiah were sitting on the porch when Canyon rode up with Club and dismounted. She got up, brushed hair out of her eyes and put out her arms for a hug.

"Well, gambler, did you win a few hands today, or did you have to fold and come back home to me?"

He hugged her and then addressed Isaiah. "Have you been teaching her gambling terms, young man?"

"No sir, she came up with that all on her own," said Isaiah.

Brenda broke away from his arms and put her hands on her hips. She looked up at the six-foot frame of her beau. She had to lift up on her toes to reach his lips since she wasn't but five-six. After one little peck on his lips, she looked at Isaiah. "Take Canyon's horse to the barn and care for it. You might as well feed and water all the animals before you come in for supper."

Isaiah got up and started down the porch steps when Canyon said, "Take your rifle with you and keep it close. I had a run-in with two more of Gaines's men when they came to examine the damage to the lake."

Brenda stomped her foot. "When were you going to tell me that you had trouble?"

"I didn't say it was trouble, and I just told you," said Canyon as he sat in the chair Isaiah had gotten up from.

"I'm sorry that I snapped at you," said Brenda as she pulled her hair out of her eyes. "All this fighting with Paul Gaines has taken its toll on me. Do you think they'll come back to the house tomorrow since he warned us to be gone by noon?"

Canyon started rocking back and forth in the rocker. The dog came onto the porch and lay between him and Brenda. Canyon thought about her question for a moment before stopping his rocking and petting his dog on its head. "I'll tell you what we should do, but you may not like it."

"I've learned that you are a calculating man, and every decision you've made has been right on. So tell me what we should do, and me and Isaiah will back you."

Canyon stood up and paced back and forth along the porch. When he stopped, he hollered out, "Isaiah, come back up to the house."

He continued his pacing until the boy was seated.

"I'm a gambler, and that's all I knew until I came here. Y'all took me in and didn't ask about my past or where I came from. My real name is Oliver Canyon Golden. I'm the man who killed Paul Gaines's boy, Jeff. I killed him in self-defense with a room full of witnesses. Brenda and Bart had suspected that it was me, and they were right."

"Canyon, Isaiah and I are glad that Jeff is dead. He killed our pa, and we despised the ground he walked on," said Brenda. "But old man Gaines has been after our land for two years."

"A good gambler sits at the poker table and studies the men sitting around it more than he does his cards. He watches their facial expressions for little signs. He can tell when they have a good hand, and when they're bluffing. He also pays close attention to their body language for signs of weakness. Money is most men's weakness. They want to avoid buckling a gambler with a habit of betting big when he thinks he'll win the hand. I don't bluff. I play the cards that have been dealt to me, and here's what I see in my hand."

Brenda took a drink from the glass that had been sitting beside her chair. Canyon reached for the glass in her hand and drank the rest of the water in it.

"Gaines made a threat yesterday that he has to follow through on, except he won't be one of the men who comes this way. He doesn't have the guts to face me again. As far as I know, he's unaware that I killed Jeff, and I want to keep it that way until the time is right. He'll send a large group of his men here, but we'll be waiting on them by the narrow valley we were at earlier today. They're high on themselves and they won't be expecting us to be the aggressor."

"When do you think they'll be coming through that part of the range?" asked Isaiah.

"Gaines will want to show his superiority and have them depart his ranch headquarters right after breakfast. We'll leave here at daylight so we can be in position in time. Each of us will have two fully loaded rifles and our handguns. We'll do our best to take out the ones in front —the front riders will be the hired guns. The rest of the group will be cowboys trying to keep a job."

"Will Chandler be with them tomorrow?" asked Brenda.

"No, Chandler will stay with Gaines, along with a few more gunfighters. He's a smart man and will most likely go into Albany tomorrow night to drink when what's left of his group goes back home like a whipped dog. After we attack them, they'll turn tail and go back to Gaines's ranch, and I want you two to come back here," said Canyon.

"Now hold on!" shouted Brenda. "What are you going to be doing?"

"I'm going to ride the creek bottom until I can see what's happening at Gaines's Hacienda."

"Why are you wanting to know what happens there?" she asked.

"When sitting at the table with a good hand, you bet and bet big. You have to be the aggressor, which will do two things to your opponent. Number one, he'll think you're bluffing and want to call, or he'll think you have finally lucked out with a good hand, and he'll fold. He doesn't understand that most hands win when you do that. He can't figure out what you're holding."

"I'm confused," said Brenda. "What're you saying?"

"I'm saying after those men go back to Gaines's ranch defeated tomorrow, that's when we start being the aggressor. I'll watch and see if Chandler goes into Albany tomorrow afternoon. If he does, I'll settle up with him once and for all. He'll be alone because the ranch can't afford to let other hands go into town with him."

"I wish you wouldn't do that," said Brenda. "Maybe he'll be with the group in the morning, and you don't have to face up to him."

"He won't be with that group. He has too much pride to ride with a gang. He wants everyone to know and fear him for his own gun. I don't fear Chandler because I know that I can kill him. I may be a gambler, but I also know how to draw and shoot with the best of them. Chandler is not in my league, which gives me an advantage over him. He doesn't know who I am and thinks he's better than me."

Brenda took a deep breath before she began to talk. "I've noticed something that you do when you feel a fight coming. You tap your index finger against the holster of your gun. Why do you do that?"

"I'm impressed you noticed that. It's a thing that I do when I play cards to intimidate people. I laid my cards on the table and tapped my finger. It causes the other players to take their minds off their cards."

Brenda sat looking up at her man, nervously wringing her hands for a few seconds. "I'm coming with you to Albany. I can't sit here and let you take on Chandler by yourself. What if he has friends there? Isaiah and I can be there to back you, and no one has to know that we're together until it's time for action."

"I don't like that idea, but I understand why you want to help," said Canyon. "Here's what we do. We go ahead and leave the house at daylight, and when the skirmish is over down by the creek, the two of you ride back to the barn and get two packhorses. You can have them ready to travel before we leave in the morning to stop the men coming this way. I'll proceed with my plan to spy on Gaines's ranch, and the two of you ride on into Albany and buy what supplies you need."

"Okay, but we need to keep watch for you so we can help," said Brenda.

"You be on the watch for Chandler, but don't get close to him or let him see you. When I get to town, we'll make contact, and you can go in the saloon and sit at a table off to the side. Don't sit near him or do anything to cause people to notice you. Pull your guns and be ready when I come through the door because I won't play around with him," said Canyon.

"Okay. It looks like we're going to be busy tomorrow. I have one more question. What're we going to do with Gaines?"

"When the time is right, we attack his hacienda and kill the man," said Canyon.

"Let's hope you have a good plan when the time comes," said Brenda. "That might be more than me, you, and Isaiah can handle."

"We'll cross that bridge when we come to it. Let's let Isaiah finish his chores, and you and I'll cook supper. It's getting late, and we have to be up early tomorrow," said Canyon.

CHAPTER THIRTY-FIVE

C anyon woke up an hour before daylight, tired from tossing and turning in his sleep. He felt like he had been awake all night but knew that wasn't so. He lay in his bed thinking about what would happen when the men from the Gaines Ranch came looking for trouble.

He knew in his heart that all the men on Gaines's payroll weren't hired guns, and he hated that some of them might get shot today. But nevertheless, they chose to work there and took on the possibility that death could come their way. They had decided to go to the Wotton range to cause harm to a woman and a boy.

Canyon got out of bed, went to the washbowl, and splashed water onto his face. Before drying off, he ran his finger along the scar on his cheek. He turned his face sideways, his scar facing away from the glass, and looked at his profile, with his brown eyes, straight nose, and smile that was known to charm. Now on the other side of his face, he could only focus on the scar that Chandler and his men had put there.

He dried off the remaining water droplets and ran a comb through his black hair. When things settled down, he'd get Brenda to cut his hair. It had gotten long since his haircut in Abilene a few weeks ago.

He put his hat on first, then the two guns he always wore, and ensured the bullet loops on his holster belt were full. He paused, lifted his head, and closed his eyes. *Lord, I'm not much on religion or praying. I know you exist, and I ask that you watch over the three of us today. Amen.*

Brenda was already in the kitchen putting together their breakfast. He stood in the doorway and watched her roll out biscuit dough. She had really grown on him these last few weeks. At first, he didn't think she was all that pretty, but now that he had spent time with her, he thought she was the most beautiful woman he had ever known. Not only was her appearance stunning, but she also had a heart of gold and was someone he thought he could ride the river with. In addition, she shot guns like she had been doing it all her life.

Brenda swung around with the roller in her hand. "That's a good way to get conked on the head. You should never startle a woman holding a roller pin."

"Sorry, I was only admiring the beauty before me," said Canyon.

"Why thank you, darling," said Brenda, smiling.

"I was talking about those biscuits you're cutting out." With that, he moved and put the table between himself and her.

"I'd come after you, but I have important work to do," she said with a laugh.

He walked around the table, put his hands around her waist, leaned over, and kissed her neck.

"You've had your fun. Now, go get a cup of coffee and let me get these biscuits in the oven," said the young woman.

Isaiah entered the kitchen, and Canyon poured the two of them coffee while Brenda finished preparing their meal. The men sipped their drinks without any conversation. It was obvious they both had something on their minds and didn't want to talk about it.

With their meal finished, Canyon glanced out the window at the back of the kitchen. "The sun is beginning to rise. Let's all hold hands while Isaiah asks for God's divine help today."

"Well, we must be rubbing off on you since you're wanting prayer," said Brenda as she reached out to hold Isaiah's and Canyon's hands.

After the prayer, the three carried their extra rifles to the barn and saddled up their horses. They rode in silence toward the location where they planned to ambush Gaines's hands.

Canyon led the way and was in deep thought, reviewing the situation. The main concern was to keep Brenda and Isaiah safe. They would have to be placed where it would be hard for Gaines's men to get to them. He was optimistic that the men they were going to encounter would get off some shots. If the three of them could get the approaching riders in a crossfire, then Gaines's men would be hit with a volley of bullets from multiple directions. If the surprised men did get off a few shots, they would most likely be shooting wild and not hitting close to anyone. The element of surprise and precision placement of those first few shots might make the difference.

Brenda brought him out of his thoughts when she rode up beside him. "I assume you want us to make sure that the first shot counts, and then we just fire among the remaining riders?"

"It's most important that the first two shots hit someone. After that, you can take your time to get a good bead on someone and then start the volley of shots. If you and Isaiah can keep them occupied long enough, I can hit three or four before they hightail it out and retreat," said Canyon.

"We'll try, is all I can say. How many of them do you think there will be?" Brenda asked.

"I'm not sure, but it can't be all that many," replied Canyon. "We've already thinned out Gaines's men. I'm hoping no more than ten total."

"Yes, but with his money, I'm sure he could hire more from Albany or one of the other small towns," said Brenda.

"Probably, if anyone wanted to work for the man. I kind of figured he already had any local help that was available," said Canyon.

"The narrow valley is over the next hill," said Isaiah.

CHAPTER THIRTY-SIX

The three riders, Canyon, Brenda, and Isaiah, stopped at the top of the hill and looked down at the creek, still full of water and running swiftly to the west.

"I suspect they'll ride along this side of the creek," said Canyon. "Isaiah, you should ride downstream and find a place to cross over and then return this way. You can hide your horse below that hill on the other side and walk to those two cedar trees. Get comfortable on your belly with both your rifles. When you see them coming, aim at one of the men closest to the creek. Make sure that the first shot empties a saddle. Do the same with your second shot."

"Yes, sir, I can do that. I best be getting in position," said Isaiah, taking off down the creek.

"Where do you want me to go?" asked Brenda.

"We'll hide our horses back down this hill, and then I want you by that cottonwood tree right over there," Canyon pointed to a tall tree not far from them. "There's enough brush around the trunk to conceal yourself. I'm going closer to the creek and hiding behind that big cedar. When they're within range of our rifles, I'll fire the first shot at the men in the middle. After that, you take out the men closest to you."

"Okay, we should probably take care of the horses and then get in our places. See how Club is sniffing the air and looking toward the range. He knows that someone is heading for us," she said.

"I'll take the horses over behind that hill and tie them up. You get in position," said Canyon as he took the reins of Brenda's horse and rode off with it trailing behind.

Canyon ran back where Brenda was lying on the ground concealed behind the tree and brush.

"I'm ready to get this started," said Brenda.

"You just make sure you stay out of sight until I start shooting," said Canyon.

"Come on, Club, you stay with me. I may need you in a few minutes." Canyon and his dog trotted to the tree he was going to hide behind. He broke off a few small limbs so he could see through the thick growth of cedar spines.

Suddenly, Club growled and the hair on his back bristled. Canyon waved at Isaiah and Brenda so they would be ready to shoot. "Boy, you stay here with me until the shooting stops. I don't want you getting hit by a stray bullet."

Nine heavily armed riders came into view. Each man wore at least one sidearm and had a rifle in their saddle boot. A hundred and fifty yards away from Canyon's position, the expedition's leader put up his arm, indicating that he wanted everyone to stop.

Canyon waited patiently and wondered what was going on. The leader turned his horse toward the creek, and the others followed. They let their animals suck up water, and then had his men regroup and start back on their way.

As luck would have it, the men let their horses walk

right into the ambush that awaited them. Canyon took careful aim at the leader, and when the man was within thirty feet of his hiding place, he squeezed the trigger and fired. He swung the rifle, worked the lever action simultaneously, and shot another man. He was about to shoot a third rider when the remaining thugs turned and went back the way they had come. He looked up the hill to Brenda, and she was still firing. He saw another man tumble off his mount.

"Club, go make sure they're dead," said Canyon as he came from behind his tree. He counted five dead on the trail in front of him, and two more to the east. Seven out of nine wasn't bad for a man, woman, and boy.

The dog went from one body to the next, sniffing and nudging them with his nose.

"Gather up all the guns and ammo that you can. We'll use a couple of their horses to carry it back to the house, and you can turn them loose on your way to Albany," said Canyon.

Brenda and Isaiah headed toward home with the rifles, pistols, and holsters tied to several horses. Canyon made sure his guns were fully loaded and took off toward the Gaines' ranch headquarters. He loped his horse most of the way but slowed when he could see the tops of the house and barn. The creek bed would be his cover as he found a location that would give him a good view of the place.

With his horse tied where it couldn't be seen, he made his way close enough to see Paul Gaines talking to the two men who had survived the massacre. He was in a rage hollering and flinging his arms in the air. He was so upset that he pulled his gun and put it in one of the men's face like he was going to shoot him. Canyon was happy to see that only three more men came out to hear the conversation. Chandler was nowhere in sight. Either he was in the house and letting Paul release his rage, or he wasn't around.

Canyon stayed hidden, hunkered down in his saddle, for almost two hours but didn't see any more of Gaines's hands. Could he and the Wottons have wiped them all out except for the five he was seeing?

He returned to his horse and stayed in the creek bed until he was out of sight of the ranch. Maybe Chandler was in Albany, as he had suspected. If he was in town, that might not be good for Brenda and Isaiah. Canyon needed to go on to town and get some information and find Chandler quick before he saw either Brenda or Isaiah. He didn't want Chandler calling Isaiah out and getting him killed.

CHAPTER THIRTY-SEVEN

C anyon walked his horse down the main street of Albany and saw Brenda's and Isaiah's mounts tied to the hitch rail to the left of the General Store. The two packhorses were tied directly in front of the store. Canyon stopped at a dress shop and tied his horse to a ring in a post by a water trough. His eyes swept the street and boardwalk as he continued to the mercantile.

Isaiah was to his left when he entered the large shop. The boy nodded and pointed discreetly to one of the aisles. Canyon turned down the aisle and saw Brenda looking at bolts of fabric.

He knew she saw him, but she never let on that she did. She put down the cloth and started up the aisle toward Canyon. "He's not in town. No one has seen him in four days."

"Okay. I'm going to the saloon to see if I can pick up any gossip. When you have everything you need, head on back and I'll catch up," said Canyon.

"Okay, you be extra careful in the saloon. You don't know if Gaines has men in there," said Brenda and walked past him and turned toward the counter.

Canyon started out of the store and when he looked at Brenda, he tipped his hat and went outside.

He mounted his horse and rode it to the saloon, leaving it right outside in case he needed to leave quickly. The visibility inside the saloon was dim, and the only light came from the two large windows and the open doorway. Two poker tables were occupied, and he recognized a couple of the men from when he had been in before.

Two men were standing at the bar, and he knew them as the two Gaines's hands he'd had a run-in with the week before. He would start with them, so he sauntered to the counter and ordered a beer. "Howdy boys, remember me?"

"Yeah, we remember you. We don't work for Gaines anymore. We're just two cowpunchers who don't want any part of his gunplay," said the man closest to Canyon.

"Let me buy you fellers a drink. I have a proposition for you," said Canyon as he motioned to the bartender to refill their glasses. "I'd like to hire you to work for the Wottons on their range. All you have to do is ranch work, no gunplay. You'll have to sleep in the barn, but I'll pay the going rate for your time."

"We don't want to be a part of this range war between you and Gaines," said one of the men.

"I expect you to protect yourself if trouble comes your way. No one will ask you to ride on Gaines's range to kill anyone. What are your names? I'm Canyon."

The man closest to him stuck out his hand to shake. "I'm Hubert Robertson, and this is Waylon Branson." Waylon stuck out his hand to shake also.

"I'm looking for someone, and I'm hoping you know where he is. I'm searching for Chandler."

"You may want to rethink that. Chandler is in a league above the rest of the gun hands at the ranch," said

Hubert. "Mr. Gaines sent him off looking for the man who killed his boy, Jeff."

"Where do you think he might be?" asked Canyon.

Waylon spoke up. "I heard Gaines tell Chandler to hit every little town between here and Abilene. He said to watch every place with poker tables because the man who killed his boy was a professional gambler. If I was a guessing man, I'd say he's at Abilene by now. Wouldn't you say that, Hubert?"

"Yep, you hit the nail on the head. He should be there by now, and if I'm a betting man, I'd wager he's with that saloon girl he usually sees when he goes there."

"What saloon girl?" asked Canyon.

"She's a little redhead who works at the Silver Spur," said Waylon.

"What kind of horse does Chandler ride nowadays?" asked Canyon.

"He rides a black horse with a big white spot on one of his hindquarters," said Hubert.

"Okay, thanks," said Canyon. "If you fellers get your horses and follow me, I'll introduce you to your new boss."

Brenda and Isaiah were mounting up when Canyon and the two cowhands rode up. "This is Hubert and Waylon. I hired them to work at the ranch as cowpunchers. This lady is Brenda, and that's Isaiah. They own the Wotton ranch, and you'll take orders from them."

"Welcome men. I'm sure we have plenty to do to keep you busy," said Brenda, and then she turned to Canyon with a questioning look.

"We'll do our darn best, boss lady," said Hubert.

"You men take the lead ropes of those packhorses, and we'll head to the house," said Canyon.

As they rode, Canyon told Brenda what the men had said about Chandler being in Abilene. He also told her he had the money to pay the two hired hands and not to worry about selling cattle to pay their wages.

When they got back to the ranch, Canyon showed the men around the place while Brenda fixed supper. After everyone got through eating supper, Isaiah, Hubert, and Waylon went outside to finish the evening chores.

Canyon took Brenda by her hands. "In the morning, I'm riding to Abilene to kill Chandler. You and Isaiah will be safe until I get back. Gaines doesn't have the manpower to come calling. He's down to five men and if some of them drag up like Hubert and Waylon did he'll be in a bind until he can hire more help."

"I wish you wouldn't go, although I know you need to. We can't go on with the threat of Chandler showing up at his leisure. But I can ride with you if you want some company," she said.

"I think this is one time I need to go by myself. I'll be fine because Chandler is overconfident, and he has no idea how fast I am," said Canyon.

CHAPTER THIRTY-EIGHT

Canyon ate breakfast with Brenda before daylight, then went to the barn for his horse.

"Boss, you're up early," said Waylon as he sat on his bed of hay and pulled on his boots.

"Yeah, I have important things to do and I want to get an early start. I'll be gone most of the day, so you and Hubert watch after Brenda and Isaiah."

"Okay, you can count on us. But I have a question about your dog. Will he bite?" asked Waylon.

"I reckon he will. Why do you ask?"

"He came into the barn last night, and when I tried to pet him, he bristled up and growled at me."

"He doesn't know you and until you and him get acquainted, I wouldn't try to pet him again," said Canyon. He started toward the door with his horse in tow. "I best be going. If you want to become friends with my dog, I suggest you feed him. He has a soft spot for anyone that gives him food."

"Okay, we'll watch out for things here, and I'll give the dog something to eat."

Canyon led his mount to the house, where Brenda

waited on him on the front porch. Club came and stood beside his horse as Brenda came down the steps. Canyon put his arms around her waist and lifted her up so their lips would touch. "I might be gone until tomorrow, so don't get in a hissy if I don't come home tonight."

"Oliver Canyon Golden, be safe and get your tail back here when you finish your business with Chandler."

"Yes, ma'am, I sure will. Give me one more kiss for the road."

Canyon left out as the sun was barely breaking the horizon, with Club following. He loped his horse until it was lathered up and needed rest. An hour later, Club wasn't in sight anymore, but he knew the dog would follow. If things worked as planned, he would go from one saloon to another looking for Chandler and find him before too long.

Canyon smiled at his good fortune in meeting Brenda. She was the woman he wanted to settle down with for the rest of his life. But before that could happen, he had to rid them of Paul Gaines and his hired guns.

He stopped at a natural water tank close to the road. His horse needed water and a few minutes of rest. He was getting back into the saddle when he heard a bark. There came Club trotting down the road after him. He waited until the dog had his fill of water before heading out.

After an hour of loping his horse, the animal threw a shoe on one of his hind hooves, and they had to go slower the rest of the way to Abilene, arriving mid-afternoon. The saloons and gambling halls were already busy by the sound of music coming out of the doorways and open windows as he rode down Main Street. Quite a few horses were tied along the busy street, and he figured a couple of herds had most likely come to town.

The first stop was at the livery stable. "Howdy, what

can I do for you?" asked the owner when Canyon dismounted.

"My horse threw a shoe on his hind hoof. Can you take care of that for me today?"

"Yep, I'll take him over to the blacksmith. I have a forge over there and can put new shoes on him. That'll be two dollars unless you want me to also feed him tonight."

"Here's three dollars. Just get him ready to ride," said Canyon. He looked down at his dog. "Come on, Club, let's go."

At the Silver Spur Saloon, Chandler was nowhere to be seen, and neither was the red-headed girl that his ranch hands had said worked there. Maybe it was too early, and they just hadn't come in yet.

He walked to the hotel across the street from the saloon, rented a room with a view of the street, and sat at the window until the sun began to set. Where was Chandler? Canyon didn't want to ask if anyone knew where he was because he wanted the element of surprise on his side.

Canyon went downstairs and out onto the boardwalk. When he saw the city marshal walking across the street, he contemplated what to do. When the marshal stepped up on the boardwalk, Canyon stopped him. "You wouldn't happen to know a man named Chandler, would you?"

The marshal reached down and removed the strap of his gun. "Yeah, I know him. Why are you looking for him?"

Canyon turned his scarred cheek toward the lawman so he could see it. "I have a little payback for him if he's in town."

"I remember you. The saloon girl found you almost dead in the alley. Chandler did this to you?"

"Yeah, Chandler and two of his cronies. I've already handled them. Now it's Chandler's time to pay for what he did."

"He ain't in town, and I don't want no trouble in Abilene," said the marshal.

"Then maybe you should tell me where he is so I can go find him. That way, there won't be any trouble in your town," said Canyon.

"You didn't hear this from me, is that clear?"

"Yeah, that's clear. Where's he at?" asked Canyon.

"A mile south of town and a quarter east is where he's shacked up with Fire, one of the saloon girls."

"Thanks. I'll leave town when my horse has new shoes."

"You do that. I don't want any trouble in my town from you or Chandler," said the lawman.

"There won't be any trouble from me, and I appreciate the information." Canyon and Club returned to the livery stable and waited until the hustler returned with his horse.

It was getting close to sundown, and he was familiar with the side road where the marshal said Chandler had gone. "Come on, Club, let's go eat. Hopefully, the horse will be ready when we return."

Canyon when inside the diner and ordered two plates of food. "Are you expecting another person, or are you just that hungry?" asked the waitress.

"One plate is for me, and the other one is for my dog that's outside," said Canyon.

"We don't serve animals in here, mister."

"No, you'll take it out there and set the plate down for my dog. He has a right to eat just like everyone else."

"I'll have to ask the boss lady about this," said the woman. She huffed off.

A large woman wearing a soiled apron came out from

the kitchen a few minutes later. "I hear you want to feed your dog?"

"Yes, ma'am, I ordered two plates of food. One for me and one for my dog that's outside. Lady, I ain't trying to cause you any trouble, but I'm a paying customer who wants to buy two plates of food. You can bring it out here, or I'll go somewhere else. It's your choice." Canyon stood up.

"It was a misunderstanding, mister. I'll go get your food and put the dog's in a bowl, if that's all right?"

Canyon nodded and the woman returned to the kitchen.

In a few minutes, the waitress brought Canyon his plate and started to the door with a bowl in her hand. When she opened the door, he watched Club look at the woman. "Sit down, boy, and eat your food," he called out to his dog.

Club sat down and the waitress pushed the bowl in front him. She came back in, wiping her hands on her apron. "I've seen that mutt around town before. I used to throw him bones out the back door."

"Yep, but he's my dog now, and he doesn't have to scrap for handouts anymore," said Canyon.

By the time they finished their meals and had walked back to the livery stable, Canyon's horse was standing in a stall, fed and wearing new shoes on all four hooves. Canyon and Club started out of town just as it was getting dark. He found the road but went slow until he could see the light of a lantern through two of the windows of the house where Chandler was supposed to be.

Showing up after dark was risky, and he didn't like how it made his stomach feel. Because of that uneasy sensation, he was about to leave when he heard coughing coming from inside the house. He was too far away to know who was sick, but he hoped it was Chandler.

Canyon backtracked until he found a buffalo wallow where he and Club could bed down for the night. It was a good thing he had brought his bedroll. Once Canyon was comfortable in his bed, Club swept around the perimeter of their hiding place. Then he came back and lay down beside Canyon.

After fifteen minutes of lying on the hard ground, Canyon sat up. "Club, we have a perfectly good bed a mile back in town. Let's go to the hotel and get a good night's sleep."

CHAPTER THIRTY-NINE

C anyon woke up when his dog put his paw on his arm. "Do you need to go outside, boy? Let me get dressed, and we'll go get something to eat. You can hold it for a few more minutes."

Since he didn't plan on staying another night at the hotel, he let the dog follow him through the lobby and out to the street. While Club was doing his business, Canyon headed to the café for breakfast. He was within a few feet of the diner's door when he saw a pony in front of Dr. Reynolds's office. It was a black horse with a white spot on its hindquarter.

"Come on, Club, breakfast will have to wait. That's Chandler's horse at the doctor's office." He removed the safety strap from his gun and began to tap his index finger on the holster as he walked closer and looked through the window of the office. There was Chandler, talking to the doctor. Canyon owed the doctor his life and wouldn't go inside after the man he was hunting. Instead, he would wait until Chandler came outside to confront him.

Canyon headed to the café and sat looking out the

window while his dog ate on the boardwalk. Finally, Chandler came outside, then removed a bag off his saddle and took it back inside. A few minutes later, he exited the doctor's office again, untied his horse, and started walking it down the street.

Canyon paid for his meal and went out on the boardwalk, watching as Chandler stopped and bent over coughing. So the hired gun was sick. When the coughing spell was over, Chandler resumed leading his horse to the livery stable. He went inside, giving Canyon time to run to the east side of the building and wait for the man he planned to face.

He could hear Chandler coughing inside the barn but continued to wait on him. A few minutes later, the hair on the dog's back bristled up, and Canyon knew the gunman was coming out. He waited until the man was out of the building, then he said, "Good morning, Chandler. Today is the day you die."

Chandler turned around to see who was talking. Canyon walked up to him and said, "I'm Oliver Golden, and I hear you're looking for me."

Chandler started to cough, and Canyon took a few steps back. He figured that it was a ploy to take him by surprise. Chandler took a deep breath of air and smiled. He went for his gun and almost had it out when the first bullet hit him in the chest. He stepped backward and smiled again before the second shot ended his life.

Canyon looked at the livery stable owner. "I assume you saw him draw first, didn't you?"

"Yep, but it doesn't matter; he had it coming. He's killed enough people to rot in hell anyway."

The town marshal came up. "I thought I told you I didn't want any trouble in my town."

"It couldn't be avoided. He drew on me, and I defended myself. The stable owner saw what happened."

"Lars, did you witness the shoot-out?" asked the marshal.

"Yep, Chandler drew first. It wasn't his day, I reckon," said the stable owner.

"Mister, I would appreciate it if you would leave Abilene. He had friends, and I don't want any more gunplay in my town," said the marshal.

"I'll be leaving as soon as I can saddle my horse," replied Canyon.

"Good. Someone go get the undertaker," said the marshal to a deputy that had just walked up.

"I'll go tell him, Marshal. I just saw him go into the doctor's office a few minutes ago," said the deputy.

"I'll go get your horse, Mr. Canyon," said Lars.

"Thanks, but I'll go help so I can leave town faster," said Canyon.

He and Club headed down the street, walking slowly enough to watch the undertaker and two more men carry Chandler's body from the street to the back of his wagon. Canyon kept going and never looked back.

The ride back to the ranch was slow-going. It was midmorning when he left Abilene, and it was already scorching hot. There were only a few places where he could water his horse and dog, so they rode slower, trying to avoid overheating. When they finally came to the tank, they had gotten water from on the way into town, he let the animals rest for a few minutes before continuing their journey home.

He saw cattle to his right grazing on the bluestem grass that was native to that part of Texas, and wondering who they belonged to, he veered off the road to have a look at their brands. They were branded as Bar W cattle, the same brand of the cows they had driven to Abilene to sell. But why were the Wotton cattle seven miles north of the house? When he had gone with the

Wottons a couple of weeks earlier, the herd was south-west of the house about two miles. He needed to talk to Isaiah about the cattle and see if he knew why they had come this far north.

Canyon got back on the road and loped his horse for the next fifteen minutes until he could see the house off in the distance, but something didn't look right. Brenda should be cooking at this time of day, but there was no smoke coming from the stovepipe in the kitchen. As he got closer, the only horses in the corral he could see were Isaiah's and the two packhorses.

Where was Brenda's horse, and where were the two cowhands he had hired?

"Club, go check out the house."

The dog took off and ran around the house. He stopped at the front screen door and used his nose to open it. Then he started to bark, and Canyon knew for sure that things weren't how they should be. He spurred his horse and headed to the house at a dead run. When he went inside, Isaiah was lying on the floor with blood on his shirt.

Canyon hollered to Club, "Go check the rest of the house and then the barn!"

Club took off out the door, while Canyon went to Isaiah. He had been beaten, by the looks of his swollen nose and eyes. The skin around his eyes had turned black, blue, and purple. Canyon pulled the boy's shirt open and found a gunshot wound in the boy's left shoulder. It looked like it had missed his heart, but it was still a severe injury.

Canyon hurried to Isaiah's bedroom and threw an old quilt over the covers. Then he went into the kitchen, threw wood in the stove, and set a large pan of water to boil.

He managed to pick up the tall, burly boy and carry

him to the bed, but the effort made his rib cage hurt where he was shot over two months ago. He cut Isaiah's shirt off with a knife from the kitchen and inspected the boy's body. His stomach and ribs were bruised and looked awful with discolored skin from the beating. Whoever had done this had intended to kill the kid, but he was still alive, and it was up to Canyon to try to keep him that way.

Canyon found some white linen cloth that he could use on the bullet wound, but he couldn't find anything to prevent infection or pain. While cleaning the area around the wound with the hot water, he thought about something his ma used to put on him and his pa when they cut themselves. She would mix together turpentine and sugar to stop the bleeding and infection. He went to the kitchen and looked around, finding an entire bottle of the awful-smelling turpentine. He put two spoons of sugar in a bowl and poured in the turpentine until it made a paste.

By the time he got back to the bedroom, the wound had bled some more, and he had to clean it off before he could make a poultice to place on the wound.

Isaiah needed a doctor, and the closest one was in Albany. Canyon needed to know what had happened and where Brenda was, but he couldn't leave Isaiah all alone, unconscious.

He went to the kitchen, took one of the chairs to the bedroom, and sat and fumed. It was likely that those two Gaines' hands had played him for a sucker and bluffed their way into his and Brenda's good graces. They had to have been a big part of whatever happened here today.

He heard a moan. Isaiah tried to open his eyes, and Canyon went to the bedside.

"Isaiah, it's me, Canyon. Can you hear me? Come on and open those eyes. I need to talk to you." He laid a wet rag on the boy's forehead and tried to wake him.

The boy said, "They hurt me badly."

"Yes, they did, but we'll get you patched up and feeling better soon. Can you tell me what happened?"

"They came and beat me and took Brenda."

"Who came and took Brenda?"

"Gaines and his men. They knew you were gone, and the two new hands weren't here."

"Does Paul Gaines have Brenda at his hacienda?" asked Canyon.

"I don't know. I'm tired now," said Isaiah, and went back to sleep.

Canyon needed to go get the doctor or take the boy to Albany. That would be quicker and save him valuable time to find Brenda.

He ran to the barn and harnessed up the two horses they had used as pack animals, readying the wagon to make the trip to Albany. Next he tied his pony to the back of the rig and parked it by the front porch.

The wagon bed would need some cushioning, so Canyon took the feather mattress off his bed and placed it in the wagon, along with a couple of quilts and a pillow. He filled two canteens and then went back to the boy.

"Isaiah, wake up. I need to replace the dressing on your shoulder and get you loaded in the wagon."

The boy didn't regain consciousness until Canyon sat him up so he could wrap the cloth around his chest and shoulder to hold the bandage.

"That hurts really bad," said Isaiah through busted-up lips.

"I wish I had something to help with the pain, but I'm almost positive there is no liquor here or any pain elixir," said Canyon.

"Look under the kitchen counter."

Canyon searched and found a half-filled bottle of whiskey. Although he never drank the stuff himself because of what it had done to his father, it would at least dull the boy's pain during the trip to town.

"Here, start drinking this while I get you in the wagon," Canyon said, handing the boy the bottle to hold in his good hand.

Isaiah was able to help get himself into the wagon bed and lie down. After a few swallows of the stout alcohol, he said, "I'll take my chances on the ride. I can't stand the taste of this stuff," and handed the bottle to Canyon.

Club jumped into the back of the wagon and lay beside Isaiah.

The horses pulling the wagon were hot and lathered up when they stopped in front of the doctor's office two hours later. Canyon had only stopped to let them get a breather once on the entire ride to Albany.

They were parked in front of a building with a sign that read, *Doctor Simmons Clinic and Sanitarium.* Canyon had to knock multiple times before the doctor finally opened up. "What do you want this time of night? It must be close to midnight, mister."

"I have Isaiah Wotton in the wagon, and he's been shot and beaten," said Canyon.

"Let's get him inside so I can tend to him."

The doctor helped Canyon get the boy onto a narrow bed in a room that he used to examine patients. Dr. Simmons cut the cloth that covered the bandage and inspected the wound. "Someone cleaned it up well, and the turpentine and sugar sure helped the bleeding. I'm not fond of it, but sometimes we have to use what we have."

"Doctor, I'll take the wagon to the livery stable while you examine Isaiah. I'll be right back," said Canyon.

"You do that. I'm going to load the boy up on laudanum, and then you and I will remove that bullet," said the doctor as he put the bottle of the pain medication to Isaiah's mouth so he could take a few swallows.

Canyon took the wagon to the livery and paid the man who was there extra to remove the harness from the animals and give them feed. He also wanted to go to the saloon and see if Hubert and Waylon were there, but he had more important things to do, like help save his friend's life.

The boy was asleep when Canyon returned at the doctor's office.

"I have him sedated, and I'm ready if you are."

Canyon walked up to the table where the boy lay, pulling up his sleeves. "What do you want me to do?"

"You put your weight on him so he can't move while I go in after the bullet. I can't have him jerking around, or I could damage him more."

Canyon laid over Isaiah's chest and held onto his left arm. The doctor took a long, slender knife and put it in the hole made by the bullet. He began to move the blade, at the same time putting another similar instrument into the wound. Isaiah tried to move, but Canyon held on.

"Here it comes," said the doctor. He picked it up out of the wound with his fingers. "It's a .36-caliber bullet, if that's any use to you." He wiped his hands clean. "Keep holding him down while I put iodine in the bullet hole and get him bandaged up. Then we'll move him to a regular bed."

Once Isaiah was resting comfortably, Canyon left the doctor's office and walked to the saloon with Club beside him.

CHAPTER FORTY

C anyon and Club stayed outside the saloon doors long enough to survey the room. He didn't see Hubert or Waylon anywhere inside.

"Club, we're going to walk in there, and I'm going to ask a few questions. So you watch my back and attack anyone who comes after me."

He pushed through the batwing doors, and the dog came in behind him. The barkeeper hollered out, "I don't allow dogs in my saloon. Get rid of him."

Canyon pulled his gun and pointed it at the man. "How about I ask you some questions, and if you don't answer them truthfully, I'll get rid of you?"

Club growled at a man sitting at a table who had moved his hand toward his gun. The man looked into the eyes of the dog. Recognizing that Club looked like he was about to take a chunk from his arm, the man carefully set his hand back on the table.

"I'm looking for Hubert and Waylon," said Canyon. "I know they've been here, and I aim to find them. I hired them to work for Brenda Wotton, but they betrayed her and gave her over to Paul Gaines. So someone had better start talking before I lose my temper."

The bartender was the first to speak. "They were here but left about an hour ago. I don't know where they went."

An older cowboy who had seen his share of sun and wind judging by the wrinkles on his face said, "I never liked those two and don't cotton to Paul Gaines. Hubert has a little shack about a half mile east of town. There's a rock on the side of the road where the house is."

"Thanks a lot, mister." Canyon turned to leave, but the dog didn't move. He stood looking at the cowboy who had started to move his hand toward his gun a few minutes ago. The dog stood ready to attack with the hair raised on his back.

"Mister, can you get your dog?" asked the man Club was watching.

"Come on, boy, we have places to go."

Club growled at the man and then turned to follow Canyon outside.

The ride to the shack the old cowboy had told him about was short. A lantern was still lit inside the house and the glow could be seen through the two open windows that had ragged curtains over the openings. Canyon tied his horse off the road so the men couldn't hear his horse's hooves approach the house. The spurs on his boot were next and he removed them and took the safety strap off his gun. Giving Brenda over to Paul Gaines had been a terrible thing to do, but he didn't want to kill them just yet. He needed answers and wanted at least one of the men alive. He had no doubt that he and Club could make one of them talk.

Canyon slowly snuck up to the one-room shack and stood beside the window to see if he could spy on the men. It sounded like they were debating where they would go the following day to get away from Albany in case the gambler happened to still be alive.

Moving closer, he peeked inside and saw that both men were in their long johns, sitting on bunks across the room from each other.

Canyon crept away from the tiny house until he was about ten feet away and lined up with the door before advancing with his gun. He kicked the door open, and the dog ran in ahead of him and jumped onto Waylon's cot.

Hubert reached for his gun, which sat on a rickety table. When he grabbed it, the table turned over and he fell onto the dirt floor. The dog bared his sharp fangs only inches from Waylon's wide-eyed face. Waylon didn't move or say anything, he knew better.

"Hubert, get off the floor and sit beside Waylon," shouted Canyon.

"Okay, don't shoot! What about that dog?"

"He's here to make sure the two of you tell me the truth. If I think either of you is lying, I'll let him eat his supper, if you get my drift."

When Hubert was seated again, Canyon called off Club and then looked at the man. "Now I want to know exactly what happened at the Wotton's and why you did what you did," he said.

"We didn't do anything wrong," said Hubert. "We saw Gaines and his men coming, and we took off."

"Yeah, we took off and don't know anything," said Waylon.

"Club, if either of these liars makes a move, bite their privates off." Canyon picked up a pair of britches off the floor, patted on the pockets and then pulled a wad of bills out of a pocket and threw it on Hubert's cot. He did the same to another pair of pants draped over the back of a chair.

"You boys were broke when you came to the ranch. Now you have a lot of money. This is your last chance to tell me the truth before I turn the dog loose on you," insisted Canyon.

Hubert raised his arm and started to point his finger at Canyon, but Club lunged at the man and bit down on his hand. Hubert screamed and tried to jerk his hand back, but the dog had his jaws clamped down tight.

"Please, get him off me! I'll tell you the truth," moaned Hubert.

"Turn him loose, boy," Canyon said to the dog. He turned to the man. "You better tell me the truth, or I'll let him start chewing on you again."

Hubert cradled his hand, which bore a fresh set of bloody teeth marks. "We overheard the woman call you Oliver. That was the name of the man who killed Jeff Gaines a few weeks ago. We rode off this morning and talked to Mr. Gaines, and he offered us five hundred dollars for our information. He paid us and we came to town. That's all we know. We didn't know he took the woman or hurt the boy. I swear we didn't know any of that."

"Waylon, do you have anything to add to his story?" asked Canyon.

"No, that's how it was."

"If you didn't have anything to do with it, how did you know Gaines took the woman and hurt the boy?" said Canyon as he moved one step closer to the two men. "No one knows that except the men who were there. You took Gaines and his men to the house and saw what they did to that boy."

"If we tell you everything, will you let us go?" asked Waylon. "We promise to leave Texas."

"I'm not going to promise you anything. You tell me

the truth, or I'll kill you. Get to talking before I start shooting your knees," said Canyon.

Waylon spoke up. "We went back to the Wotton's place and kept Brenda and Isaiah occupied until Gaines and his men could surround the house and come inside. The boy tried to put up a fight but was no match for Gaines. He's the one who beat the boy and shot him."

"How many men did Gaines have with him?" asked Canyon.

"It was him and five men. That's all he has left," said Waylon.

"Was he taking her back to his hacienda?" asked Canyon.

"Yeah, and they're waiting on you to show up there. Gaines has her in the small shack out behind the main house. His men are waiting on you in the main building. That's all I know, I swear," said Waylon.

Canyon stood staring at the two men for a few seconds, debating what to do next. "You two get on your horses and ride as fast and as far away as you can before I change my mind. If I ever see either of you again, I'll kill you on the spot. Is that understood?"

"We understand," said Waylon, and he reached for his shirt on the back of a chair.

"No, you don't understand," said Canyon. "I said get on your horses and leave now. That doesn't mean you have time for clothes, guns, saddles, or bedrolls. You men did the Wottons and me wrong, and I'm letting you live. Time's a-wasting. Get on those horses and be gone."

"Can we at least take our boots?" asked Hubert.

"No. Get going before I turn the dog loose on you," said Canyon.

The two half-dressed cowboys went to their horses and put bridles on them. They complained about not having their boots, and having to step in lord knows what in their stocking feet.

When both men sat bareback on their ponies, Canyon said to Club, "Go get 'em, boy!" The dog ran after the horses and started to bite their hind legs, causing them to kick and buck. The horses took off running to get away from the dog.

Canyon went inside and picked up the money he'd found in their pockets. He carried the lantern to the door and threw it against the wall, breaking the glass and spilling kerosene on one of the cots. The shack caught on fire and burned with the two men's possessions still inside.

Canyon and Club stayed long enough to watch the shack burn to the ground. He didn't want to leave until he was sure that everything that the two men owned was burned.

CHAPTER FORTY-ONE

All the lights were turned off in Dr. Simmons's office when Canyon and Club got back to town and rode on by the sanitarium. Him and the dog continued down the street and headed to the Rocking G Ranch to scope out the place so he could figure out a plan to rescue Brenda. Gaines's ranch was six miles west and eight north, but if he rode across country at an angle, he could get there quicker since it was dark and likely no one would see him.

Hubert and Waylon had said the men were located in the house and Gaines was holding his girlfriend in a different building. That would make it more challenging to go in there on his own.

Those two had lied to him earlier and betrayed the Wottons, so he didn't rely on the information they had provided to be accurate. He needed to see for himself. He'd get as close as he could to the ranch building. The moon wasn't up yet and it would be hard for anyone to see him or Club, which was an advantage.

When he was within a half mile of the Rocking G Ranch, he left the road and found the creek bed again. It was lower than the surrounding landscape, so he could stay hidden until he was close enough to dismount and get closer to the structures and yard.

It was a good thing that he'd been there before because the hacienda, barn and other buildings were hard to distinguish in the darkness. The way the streambed ran gave him the location he remembered where he had left his horse the other two times he had watched the ranch headquarters.

After moving in closer, he squatted on his haunches and petted the dog. "Boy, they're going to be ready to shoot us if they get a chance."

Suddenly he heard the hooves of running horses heading toward the main house. Canyon stayed hidden.

"Hello in the house! It's Hubert and Waylon. We have information for Mr. Gaines."

Canyon watched as a lantern was lit in the barn and kerosene lamps shone in the windows of the hacienda. The barn door opened and two men armed with rifles walked out, standing ready to engage in a fight. One man came out onto the porch and talked to the two men still on their horses. Another man rushed out the door of the house and pointed his rifle at the two men.

The two men in front of the barn joined the others on the porch, wanting in on the conversation. Canyon couldn't hear what was being said, but the exchange between the men gave him time to move toward the barn.

Canyon and Club quickly went into the barn and found a location where they could hide when the two men came back in. He would wait until they were ready to blow out the lantern and then kill them. He wouldn't have time to question them or make sure they were dead; he would have to get away as quickly as possible. At the back of the barn was another door—he crept over to it and opened it a few inches so he could sneak out when he was done. That would also give him access to the house. He could exit the barn from the back and run to the back of the house without being seen.

Gunshots filled the silence of the night air. Three shots echoed from the front of the hacienda, then a fourth. Canyon peered out the door and saw that someone had brought out a lantern. There stood four of Gaines's men, holding their guns. He could make out two corpses on the ground. He pulled back into the darkness of the barn before someone saw him. Hubert and Waylon must have demanded money for their information, and it had gotten them killed.

Canyon waited patiently inside the barn with his gun ready to fire. After a few minutes, he heard talking, and the conversation was getting closer to the barn. He was ready. The shadows of two men walked past the barn door and in a few minutes they came back leading a horse. They must have gone to the corral, thought Canyon. One of the men came inside the barn and took some rope off a peg on the wall. He went back outside, and the sound of their steps grew faint.

Shortly thereafter, he heard the sound of horse hooves and the noise of something being dragged across the gravel in front of the barn. He could see just enough to know what it was. The two men were dragging the bodies away from the house. The coyotes would have a feast tonight and the buzzards tomorrow.

It seemed to take forever for the men to come back into the barn. Only it was three men instead of two. One of them went to a chest, opened the lid, and pulled out a bottle of whiskey. When he turned it up to take a swallow, Canyon made his move.

"Hello, boys," he said, and shot the man closest to the door. As he turned his gun on the second man, Club came from his hiding place and leaped off a stack of hay, hitting the man with the whiskey bottle square in the chest.

Canyon and the third gun hand exchanged bullets. The other man lost.

Then Canyon ran to Club, who had the man with the bottle on the ground. But there was no need to do more shooting. The dog had bitten straight into the man's throat and he had already bled to death.

"That's three down, Club. We have three more to go. Let's go out the back door and see if we can get into the house." Canyon rubbed his dog's head. The lone man in the house would most likely be waiting on them and not come to the barn, even though he probably heard the gunshots and knew there'd been trouble. Canyon blew out the lantern before making his way out of the back door of the barn.

"Club, we're going to the house as fast as we can. You go to the back door and I'll go to the front. If you see someone, attack to kill," he whispered.

Canyon took off running and the dog passed him, going as fast as he could to the front of the house instead of the back. The dog stayed on the porch barking and clawing at the front door until Canyon had reached the side of the house, where he was safe.

Club quit barking and came off the porch. He looked up at the second floor with the hair on his neck standing up straight. Canyon knew what that meant. Whoever was in the house had taken up a position upstairs. He stayed close to the wall and when he came to the railing around the porch, he climbed over it.

The dog stood beside the door as Canyon pushed it open. He wasn't expecting an ambush, but still used caution. He motioned to the dog and said, "Go check out the rest of the house."

The dog practically crawled as he went hunting from room to room. Canyon found the stairs and stood beside them until the dog returned. They made it to the first landing together, until the dog took off up the rest of the stairs. Canyon followed at a slower pace, holding his gun ready to fire. When he was high enough up the steps to see the second floor, there was the dog standing beside a door, staring at it as if ready to fight. Canyon squatted beside the door, turned the knob, and pushed the door open. The dog lunged into the room. Shots rang out and splinters of wood flew off the doorframe. Whoever was inside had been taken by surprise by the dog and had fallen to the floor. Club stood over him snarling, his sharp teeth ready to shred the man's face.

"Good job, Club. Get up, mister. We have some talking to do," said Canyon.

"You keep that crazy dog away from me," said the man.

"You're in no position to tell me what to do. Where's Gaines and the girl?"

"I don't know. He didn't say where he was going."

"Fine, you're a dead man. Dog, tear out his throat," said Canyon, and the dog came forward.

The man put his hands to his throat. "I really don't know where they went. He has Willie Eastwood with him and that's all I know," the frightened man whimpered.

Canyon put his hand on the dog's head for a second. "Does Gaines have another house on the property somewhere?"

"No, not that I know of."

"I've heard of cowboys living in line shacks during the winter. Are there any of them on the property?"

"There are two of them. One is south of here about four miles and the other one is east. I've never been to that one."

"Come on, Club, it's time to go." Canyon turned to walk out of the room but suddenly turned back and fired at the man just as he was picking up his gun to shoot Canyon in the back. "I could see it in your eyes—you, sir, were not a good gambler." He grabbed the man by his boots and dragged him down the stairs and out into the yard. The buzzards would have plenty of food for a few days.

Canyon and Club went back into the house and started going through the kitchen looking for food. Neither he nor the dog had eaten since early that morning and it must have been close to midnight by now. Canyon stoked the fire and fried up slices of sugar-cured ham and scrambled a skillet of eggs. When he and the dog had filled their stomachs, he went down to the creek, got his horse, and took it to the barn to feed. They spent the rest of the night inside the house because tomorrow would be a hard day.

CHAPTER FORTY-TWO

The darkness was giving way to daylight when Canyon and Club left the Rocking G Ranch headquarters. The dog ran back and forth in front of Canyon's horse, sniffing at the ground trying to pick up the trail of Gaines and Brenda. There were so many horse tracks around the ranch headquarters that he couldn't pick up Brenda's scent, and Canyon couldn't tell by the tracks which one was her horse since they were too numerous to follow. He was hoping that once they were far enough away from the ranch, he would find tracks that he could follow.

A mile from the barn and house, they came across a trail that went in the direction of the line shack to the south. He urged his horse to go faster, and in another two miles, he topped a hill and saw the shotgun shack sitting on the banks of a stream.

"Go check it out, boy," he said. Club took off and made a circle around the crudely built line shack without acknowledging that anyone was there. Canyon couldn't imagine two men spending the winter in the tiny house. It had cracks between the boards on the outside walls and was missing a few of the cedar roof shingles. He pulled his gun and walked to the door. After taking a deep breath, he cocked the hammer, lifted the latch and pushed the door open. The old rotten leather hinges that were attached to the door broke and the door slammed onto the dirt floor. Club came running and went past Canyon barking. Canyon crouched in the doorway ready to shoot since he thought the dog had seen someone.

The dog sat on his hindquarters looking at him in despair because the small room was empty. "Come on, boy. Let's get my horse and go to the creek for a drink before we leave here."

The horse and the dog drank water from the branch of the stream behind the shack while Canyon drank from his canteen.

Canyon knew Gaines had a plan to draw him out so he could kill him. It wasn't Brenda that he wanted; she would be safe as long as he was still alive. Gaines was used to having his way and being the big rancher in this part of the country. If he lived through this, he would hire additional cowboys and gun hands to take more land. *If that happens, he will only get stronger and no one will be able to stop him*, Canyon thought. He had to find Brenda and then put a stop to Paul Gaines.

Where would Gaines take Brenda? Canyon pondered this, coming to the conclusion that he would most likely take her to her own house. Gaines probably knew Canyon would go there and use it as his home base while looking for his girlfriend.

"Come on, boy, we're going home."

He rode his horse hard until they came to the Wotton's blown-out creek dam that he had helped build. Three sets of horse tracks were very visible in the dirt, and one of them made deep imprints in the soft creek bottom soil. He figured one track was Gaines, since he was a big, heavy man. The other two sets of tracks were like one horse was behind the other. The man with Gaines must be leading Brenda's horse and that was why the tracks looked the way they did.

Canyon walked his horse in the creek bed until he could see the gully that Weasel had used to spy on the house. "Club, you stay with me. We're going up this gully to watch the house. I can't have you wandering off by yourself." The dog wagged his tail like he understood every word.

With his horse tethered in the same place that Weasel had used, Canyon continued up the gully until he had a good view of the house. He could see movement inside the kitchen every once in a while through a back window, and smoke was rising from the stovepipe. Brenda must have been in there cooking. She was probably doing it so he would see the smoke and know she was there. But who was with her? There was no way Gaines would let her stay in there by herself, so either Gaines or some of his men must be in the house with her.

After forty minutes watching the back of the house, Canyon advanced up the gully. It got shallower the farther he went, he crawled on his stomach far enough so he could see the front of the house. Brenda's horse was tied to one of the porch posts. Gaines and the man with him must have put their horses in the barn to make anyone that rode up think that Brenda was alone. The back screen door slammed, and he scurried back down the gully in time to see the gun hand walk to the barn. There was someone here other than Gaines waiting on him to show up.

Canyon found himself a comfortable position lying on his belly on the ground with the rifle to his shoulder. The man exited the barn and was almost to the house when Canyon said, "Go get him, boy!"

The dog shot out of the gully running as fast as he could toward the man. The gun hand pulled his pistol and stopped to shoot, but never had a chance because a bullet from Canyon's rifle hit him in the face and ended his life.

Club kept running and continued to the back screen door, breaking through it and tearing into the kitchen. Canyon was running toward the house when he heard cursing and a single shot. As he entered the kitchen, he saw Brenda hugging Club to her chest.

"He's in there," she said, pointing to a closed door that led to the living room. Canyon started to the door, but the sound of Brenda's horse leaving stopped him in his tracks. Instead, he ran to the front door. The big man was heading north. Canyon fired a couple of shots but missed.

He ran back into the kitchen. "Gaines took your horse and lit out. Are you hurt?" he asked as he helped her up and looked into her eyes.

"No, I'm fine. But how is Isaiah and where is he?"

"He's at Dr. Simmons's office in Albany. He took a bullet to his left shoulder and fortunately the doctor was able to remove it. Gaines worked him over pretty good with his fist and left the boy with a lot of bumps and bruises too, but he'll be okay in a few months."

"Canyon, Gaines is obsessed with killing you and will go to any lengths to do it. You'll have to kill him, or he'll hire more men to come for you," said Brenda.

"Yeah, I know. Right now, I need for you to pack a bag with enough clothes for a few days. We're riding into Albany so you can be with Isaiah. Club will stay with you, and I guarantee you that no one will harm you or Isaiah as long as he's alive."

She reached down and petted the dog. "He came through that screen door with blood in his eyes. If Gaines hadn't run to the other room, my big hairy boy would have torn him apart."

"I'm going to the barn and saddle you that other feller's horse since Gaines has yours and then we'll head out. Club, stay in here with Brenda."

About halfway to Albany, Canyon said, "I've been pondering about something. When this is over with Gaines, I think we should get hitched."

Brenda pulled back on the reins and stopped the horse she was riding. "It's about time you started thinking about marriage. I was wondering if you would ever ask."

He smiled. "The way I see it, I have a pat hand and it's time to bet it all and take home the winnings. Come on, we need to get to town."

"Always a gambler, Oliver Canyon Golden," said Brenda, laughing.

CHAPTER FORTY-THREE

I saiah was propped up in his bed when Brenda and Canyon entered his room. The nurse had placed pillows between his head and the iron bed rails so he could sit upright and eat and drink water comfortably.

"Well, little brother, I see that you're nice and comfortable in your bed. I think it's about time for you to get home and catch up on your chores," said Brenda.

Isaiah tried to smile, but the scabs on his lips restricted the movement of his mouth.

He wasn't able to part his lips but a little since his jaw was bruised and sore. "Canyon, did you get Gaines and the polecats that did this?" asked the injured boy.

"I got them all except Gaines, and now that Brenda is here with you and both of you are safe, I'll be on his trail first thing in the morning. Have you been up and moving around?" asked Canyon.

"Yeah, I get up and walk around in this room every couple hours. I swear it hurts like the dickens. I think even my hair is sore," said Isaiah.

Brenda went to his bedside and looked at the cuts and

bruises on his face. "Do you need for me to get you anything?" she asked.

"No, I'm fine for now. The doctor has me on soft food since my jaws are so sore."

She began to rearrange his covers. "Sister, I'm going to be fine. Take a seat. If I need something, I'll let you know."

Canyon went to Brenda's side and put his arm around her shoulder. "I'm going to the hotel and rent you a room for the next four days. I'll stay in town tonight, but in the morning I'm heading out to find Paul Gaines. He'll only get stronger the longer we wait."

"As much as I hate to admit it, you're absolutely right about that. I suspect he's gone to Abilene to recruit more hired guns to come after you," she said.

"That's what I'm thinking. I'll be back directly."

Canyon rented himself a room for the night, and Brenda one for five days. He took his horse to the livery to get it fed, watered, and rubbed down. His mount would need to be fresh tomorrow so he could get to Abilene before noon. He doubted Gaines would be able to recruit any help tonight since it would be late before he arrived in the cow-buying town.

Back at the doctor's office, he lingered until it was almost dark before he and Brenda went for supper at the diner. Club stayed outside and found a good place to lie while waiting for his food. Canyon took the dog a plate and went back inside to eat his own meal. While Brenda was waiting on him to finish his coffee, she asked, "Were you serious about us getting hitched when this thing is over with Gaines?"

"Yep, and I had another thought today. When Gaines is dead, what do you think about me and you commandeer the Rocking G and changing the name to whatever you want? It's a massive piece of land. Isaiah could operate the home place, and the three of us could have one of the biggest cattle operations in Texas."

She sat there looking at him in shock, her mouth open.

"Brenda, close your mouth before a fly comes to visit."

"I'm sorry, I wasn't expecting that at all. You really have been doing a lot of thinking lately, haven't you?" She reached out to take his hand. "If that's what you want to do once we're married, then I'm with you all the way. We make a pretty good team and I just want to spend the rest of my life with you, Gambler Canyon."

"I want to settle down and have a family that I can enjoy, I've traveled from one town to another playing cards and dodging bullets, and I'm tired of running from trouble."

He put some money on the table, and they started back to the hotel. "Can we walk around town before we retire for the night?" said Brenda. "It's a lovely evening, and maybe we can even window-shop for a wedding ring."

"Sure, let's get Club and we'll start moseying around town," said Canyon.

They passed a few townsfolk as they strolled holding hands along the boardwalk. At the Bank of Albany, they crossed the street. Canyon looked back. "Is that the bank Bart used?"

"Oh no, he wouldn't set foot in that bank. The banker is friends with Paul Gaines. Grandpa used one in Abilene for the few times he needed help," said Brenda.

"We'll have to find us a bank in the future," said Canyon.

They walked around town until it was time to bed down for the night. "I probably won't see you in the morning. I want to be on the trail after Gaines by daylight," said Canyon. "I'll leave the dog here with you and he'll protect you in case there's trouble."

"No, he'll be of more use to you as you track down Gaines. For some reason I don't think that awful man has gone far," said Brenda.

"I tend to agree with you. And if everything goes right, I think Club might be able to pick up his trail easier than me." Canyon held the door open for her as they entered the hotel.

When the two lovers were on the first floor, they exchanged good night kisses and went to their rooms for the evening.

Canyon and Club were on the road to Abilene before daylight. He had to saddle his horse in the dark at the livery stable since no one was there yet. At least the early mornings were cool, but that would soon change when the sun came up.

He had been on the road a little over two hours when he got the strong feeling that something wasn't quite right. Brenda had said that she didn't think Gaines had gone far. Maybe that was it. Or maybe he didn't go to Abilene and wanted Canyon to think he did. But why would he do that?

Suddenly Canyon pulled back on the reins. Gaines had gone to Albany. All his money was in the Bank of Albany, and he would be there to withdraw a large sum to pay for more hired guns.

Canyon turned around, put the spurs to his horse, and headed back to town. Hopefully the bank wouldn't open until nine, but that was wishful thinking when most banks opened at eight. It had to be close to that time now.

How would Gaines hire more gunmen? There weren't any in Albany that met those qualifications. He'd have to send out telegrams, probably all the way to Fort Worth, which was the largest town east of there.

He pushed his horse hard until they arrived back in town and left his pony at the livery.

Sure enough, the bank was open, and Canyon walked into the lobby. A fat, bald man dressed in a suit sat at a desk inside one of two offices. His door was open, so Canyon said, "Hello, I'm Oliver Golden, and I'm looking for Paul Gaines. Was he here earlier?"

"I'm sorry, but I'm a busy man. You, sir, need to leave immediately," said the banker, who was red-faced with beads of sweat forming on his forehead, either from anger that Canyon was here—or fear.

Canyon stepped inside the office, shut the door, and pulled his gun. "I don't think you heard me. Are your ears stopped up? If they are, I'll unstop them with the barrel of this gun. Now, you can answer my question immediately, or I'll beat it out of you."

"Sir, I do not give in to barbaric threats. I am a respected man in town and I will not let some stranger intimidate me."

Canyon took two quick steps forward and hit the man across his nose, causing blood to stream over his lips and drip off his chin onto his shirt. "The next one will knock your teeth out," he said, as he pulled his hand back to hit the man a second time.

"No, wait. He was here about an hour ago," said the banker, putting his handkerchief to his nose.

"How much money did he withdraw from his account?" asked Canyon.

"Three thousand dollars."

"Did he say where he was going when he left here?" Canyon made ready to hit the man again.

"He was going to the telegraph office to wire a couple of men. They're supposed to stop here when they get to town. Paul said he would be back in a couple of days to give me more instructions," said the frightened banker.

"I'm going to kill Gaines and take his ranch as my own. When I do, you might want to sell out and find another town to do business in," said Canyon and opened the office door and left the bank.

He walked to the telegraph office. The door was unlocked, but when he entered the small room, no one was around. A wooden tray sat on a shelf behind the counter, filled with a stack of paper. Canyon peered closer, reading the writing on the top piece of paper. It was the one he was looking for. Gaines had sent a message to a man by the name of Judd Walker in Fort Worth.

I have a job. Bring help. Pay is $1000. Go to the Bank of Albany for instructions.

P Gaines.

Canyon knew Judd personally; they had played cards a few times in the past and were friendly with each other.

"Hello, anyone here?" he called out as he began writing his own message on a piece of blank paper on the counter.

A man in a suit came in from the back room. "Yes, sir. Do you want to send a telegram?"

"I do." He handed the piece of paper to the operator. "Send this to Judd Walker in Fort Worth." The message read:

Don't come to Albany. Gaines is dead and no one to pay you.

Oliver Golden.

The operator's hands started to shake and he looked white as a sheet. "If I send this and Mr. Gaines finds out, he'll tar and feather me something bad."

"You don't have to worry about Gaines. He'll never find out because I'm hunting him down today for murder. Now send the message."

The man tapped the key and by the time he was

finished, his face was covered in sweat. "What if I get a reply?" asked the man.

"Take it to the hotel and leave it at the desk for Brenda Wotton."

Canyon left and went back to the stable for his horse.

CHAPTER FORTY-FOUR

Once again Canyon and Club utilized the creek bed to gain access to the Rocking G Ranch headquarters. As he settled into position, he saw Paul Gaines on a Sorrel horse, dragging off the dead bodies that Canyon had left in the yard. He must have put Brenda's horse in the barn. There must have been twenty buzzards flying in circles up in the sky, ready to feast on the decaying flesh. The bodies were probably stinking by now, or the big man wouldn't be spending his time dragging them away from the house.

Club kept looking up at the big black vultures, his hair raised on his back. Canyon reached down and petted the dog's head. "I know you want to chase after them, but you can't this time. You stay still and we'll move soon." The dog stayed beside his master, waiting until he gave the next order.

It took Gaines about ten minutes before he returned to the ranch house's yard. This time he rode to the barn and went around the side of it, and Canyon lost sight of him. A couple minutes after, his horse was pulling the two men away that Canyon and Club had killed in the barn.

Gaines had the rope tied to the men's legs and dragged them in the same direction as he had the other men. His poor horse was working hard to support the weight of Gaines plus the two corpses.

Canyon waited until Gaines disappeared from view as he descended into a small gully. It was time to leave his hiding place and run toward the house with the dog beside him. When he entered the hacienda, the first things he noticed was a stack of money on the divan in the living room, and two rifles laying on the table in front of the couch.

Canyon climbed up the stairs and went to a bedroom that had a window where he could watch the back of the residence. Gaines could be seen off in the distance and it looked like the man had dismounted and was shoving the bodies into a ravine. It became apparent that he wasn't even going to cover the corpses, as he mounted back up and coiled up the rope he had been using.

Canyon went back downstairs and watched as Gaines went to the barn, unsaddled his horse, and turned it into the corral. As he started to head back to the house, Canyon saw him look east toward the creek. Then he turned and rushed into the barn. What was he up to? Had he seen something down in the creek bed?

Canyon went to another window in the living room and what he saw made his heart skip a beat. His horse was grazing down by the creek! It must have come untied and did what horses always did—look for something to eat. While Canyon thought about what to do, Gaines came out of the barn on a different horse, galloping it back toward town.

Canyon grabbed a rifle off the divan and ran out into the yard, firing at the fleeing man. When the rider was out of firing range, he dropped the rifle and ran toward his horse. The dog took off after Gaines.

By the time Canyon joined the pursuit, Gaines was almost out of sight. Canyon knew the big man's horse couldn't keep running at the pace they were going for long, and he would be able to catch up soon. As the distance began to shorten between them, he saw Gaines turn south. Canyon went ahead and turned, hoping to cut across the terrain and catch up quicker.

Club was nowhere in sight as Canyon continued to gain ground. The evil man's horse was tiring, and he turned in the saddle enough to start firing at Canyon with his pistol. But he was still too far away, and his bullets landed nowhere close to his pursuer.

Gaines's horse was slowing down even more now, unable to keep its previous pace. As he got closer, Canyon could tell that the rancher was trying to reload his pistol. The trail they were on took them between a cut about two feet deep between two small hills. Club ran up onto the top of one of the hills and leaped at the horse and rider, landing with enough force to make Gaines almost fall to the ground. The horse felt the shift of weight and fell onto his side, pinning Gaines's right leg. The horse tried to get back up but was too tired.

Club picked himself up off the ground. He was still dazed from the impact, but made his way toward Gaines, his teeth bared, ready to attack the man.

"Club, stay," Canyon called out and dismounted.

He walked up to Gaines, who was pushing on the pony's neck in an effort to free his leg from underneath the horse. Canyon reached down and picked up the gun the man had dropped. He flipped open the latch and checked to see if it was loaded. There were two shells in the cylinder that hadn't been fired.

Canyon grabbed hold of the saddle horn of the downed horse and lifted. "Pull your leg free while I lift up," said Canyon.

With some struggle, the man freed his leg and stood up on shaky legs. He looked at Canyon. "Why did you just save my life?"

"I didn't. I wanted you up and facing me when I kill you. I killed your boy in self-defense, and that's the way I'm going to kill you."

Canyon handed Gaines his pistol by the barrel. "Put this in your holster. There're two bullets left in it. You know, you had the world in the palm of your hand until you got greedy and wanted the whole range. You let Jeff kill Bart's son and run roughshod over everyone he came into contact with. You had your hired men beat Bart to death. You personally shot the kid, Isaiah. Then you came for me. That was your biggest mistake. And Chandler was no match for me, just like your overbearing son was no match. So today you die, and I'll be the new owner of the Rocking G Ranch."

"No one, and especially not a no-good gambler, is taking my ranch," said Gaines, red-faced and spewing saliva as he spoke. "I'm going to kill you right here today, and then I'm killing those two squatters. No one will stand up to me after today."

Canyon was about to reply when Gaines made his move and surprised the gambler.

Paul Gaines was faster than Canyon had expected. The man had pulled his gun and had it nearly in firing position when the first slug from Canyon's gun hit him in the chest. Gaines dropped his gun but staggered toward Canyon with his fist clenched in anger. "I'll kill you with my bare hands," said the hurt, angry man as he lurched closer.

Canyon was walking backward when he fired another bullet to the chest of the big man and slowed his advance, but Gaines regained his momentum and started forward again. Canyon took careful aim and the third shot hit him right between the eyes. The big man wilted to the ground and fell on his face, dead.

Club ran up to the man and smelled him before he moved away and sat down. Canyon searched Gaines's back pocket but didn't find anything, and then with all his strength turned the big man over and continued to search. He removed a roll of bills and five double eagles.

Canyon rubbed his dog on the head. "Go lie down, boy. It's time I have a talk with Jesus, and it may take a while."

Canyon got on his knees, looked up at the sky, and began to pray.

Lord, I don't know what to say, but I'm going to pour out my heart to you. I've done a lot of bad things in my life and I sure would like for you to forgive me of my iniquities and cleanse me of all my sin. I know from reading your Word when I was younger that you sent your Son to die on a cross and shed his blood for me. I accept him as my Lord and savior and ask that you change me from a gunfighter to a peaceful loving man. Amen.

When he was finished, he whistled for the dog. "Come on, let's go to town and see Brenda and Isaiah."

CHAPTER FORTY-FIVE

C anyon arrived in Albany and tied his horse in front of Dr. Simmons's office and small hospital. He was tired from the ride but hopeful to find his fiancée inside.

"Club, find you a cool spot and stay here while I check on Isaiah," said Canyon. He went inside the office and infirmary, which consisted of a large room with divider curtains where there were four beds for patients. He could hear talking coming from the area where he had last seen the hurt boy. When he looked in, Brenda was washing off her brother's forehead with a damp rag. Canyon stood in the doorway watching.

After a few seconds, he cleared his throat and she turned toward him. Poor Isaiah got the brunt of her excitement as she dropped the rag onto his face and ran to Canyon. They embraced and kissed.

Then she broke away and looked into his eyes. "Is it over with for good?"

"Yep, and we're the owners of one of the biggest estates and ranges in West Texas. Why are you putting that rag on the boy's face? Does he have a fever?"

"He felt a little warm and I wasn't doing anything else, so I tried to keep his forehead cool."

"In other words, you were bored and needed something to do?" asked Canyon, smiling at her.

"That pretty much sums it up. What are your plans now that we own all those cattle?"

"I think I'll go to the saloon and see if there are any cowboys that need a job, and maybe have a beer or three. If I can't find someone who needs a job, then I may send out a couple of telegrams—one to the Fort Worth cattle buyers and another to the cattle pens in Abilene, informing them that we're hiring cowhands."

"I wish I could go with you to have a beer. It's such a dumb rule about women not being allowed in the saloons," said Brenda.

"Is that a law around here? I see women in the saloons all the time. If you want to tag along, then come on. I'll enjoy your company way more than that bunch of cowboys, drifters, and lollygaggers drinking rotgut."

"Let me wash up and we can go," said Brenda.

"Isaiah, how are you doing?" asked Canyon.

"I'm really sore and my shoulder hurts really bad at times. Sister told me your plans on taking over the Rocking G Ranch."

"I hope you're in agreement with it. You can stay at your home place, or you can come live with us. The decision is yours."

"I want to come live with you all until I'm well, and then we'll see."

"Fair enough. We best be going. I'll have Brenda back later," said Canyon.

They strolled hand-in-hand to one of the drinking establishments. Canyon felt her hand get a little sweaty in his, and she shook from nervousness. He gave her hand a light squeeze and said, "If you're uncomfortable about going in, I can do this later."

"No, I want to do this and have me a beer along with my man."

Canyon didn't want to laugh but suspected that she might be in for a surprise when she took a drink of chalk. They went through the door, and he guided her to a table where she sat down. He continued to stand, so he could address all the bar patrons. There were only about ten men in the room sitting at three different tables, and they were all looking at him and Brenda. The waitress came over to take their order. "What can I get you folks?"

"We'll each have a beer," said Canyon.

When the bar girl had left, Canyon said, "I'm Oliver Canyon Golden and I killed Paul Gaines and all his hired gun hands. Me and my soon-to-be wife have taken over the Rocking G Ranch and are hiring cowhands. If any of you need work or know of someone that does, have them come to the ranch. I won't hire any gunslingers, just cowboys."

Two men who sat at a table by themselves got up and came to Canyon and Brenda's table. "We used to work for Gaines as cowboys but quit when he had that old man beat to death. We'd like to come to work for you, mister."

The saloon girl brought the foamy mugs of chalk to the table and put them down.

"Bring two more for our friends here, if you don't mind," said Canyon. "Have a seat and let's get acquainted." Canyon took a big swallow of his beer and Brenda did the same. She grimaced when she swallowed the bitter liquid. "Well, what do you think of beer?" asked Canyon.

"It may be one of those things that a person has to acquire a taste for. I'll give this mug the benefit of the doubt before I decide if I ever want another."

Canyon turned to the two men. "What are your names?"

The man to his left pushed his hat back a little, and Canyon was able to see his face in the dim light. "I'm Luther Albertson. I think I'm thirty-two years old and was reared in Clayton, New Mexico. I pride myself in being a cowboy and will ride for the brand."

The waitress came with the two beers for the cowhands. The other man, who sat to Brenda's right, took a swallow and set his mug back on the table. "I'm Gabriel Meadows, and I grew up in north Texas, close to Paris. I'm twenty-six and Luther has been teaching me how to be a cowboy."

"It's good to have the two of you on board with us. Luther, I'm going to make you the ramrod—that is, if you'll have the position. I don't know squat about cows or anything when it comes to running a ranch," said Canyon. He looked over at Brenda, who had drained the last of the beer from her glass. He smiled and said, "I don't think you need another one of those. I'm afraid I'll have to carry you out of here now."

Her voice was a smidgen slurred when she said, "I'm fine. Let me sit here a few minutes and catch my breath."

Canyon scooted his chair a little closer to her just in case she got off balance from drinking the beer too quickly. "I'll pay thirty a month to the hands, and forty to you, Luther. If that's agreeable, let's shake on it to confirm the deal."

Both men nodded their heads and stuck out their hands.

"Luther, how many cowboys do you think we need to manage the Rocking G herd plus the other thousand that are on the Wotton place?"

"Six to eight ought to be enough to manage both places. We can always hire temporary hands or ask the neighbors to help with cattle drives and brandings if we need to," said Luther. "I know a man in Fort Worth who might be looking for a job. He's a little older than us, I'd guess maybe fifty, but he's a heck of a hand and can probably bring a few more men with him if he's interested."

"That sounds good to me. We were going to the telegraph office next to send out inquiries to the cattle pens in Abilene and Fort Worth, but it sounds like we might not have to."

"Speaking of Abilene, did you know that Chandler lives there?" asked Luther.

"Chandler is six feet under and not a threat to anyone," said Canyon.

Luther nodded and drained his glass. "Gabe, finish off that beer. We need to go with the boss to the telegraph office to get in touch with Weldon."

While the two new hands sucked down the last of the suds from their mugs, Canyon helped Brenda to her feet. She took a step and fell into his arms, giggling.

He put his arm around her back and took hold of her arm with his other hand. "Come on, one step at a time, sugar."

They made it to the door and onto the boardwalk. Canyon stopped long enough to say, "Go on to the telegraph office and send your message to the man you know. I'll take her to the hotel and meet you there."

A few people gave Brenda questioning looks as she walked with unsteady legs on the boardwalk toward the hotel. Once inside the lobby, Canyon picked her up in his arms and carried her to the room he had rented for her on the first floor. He laid her on the bed and said, "I'll be back directly, and we'll go get something to eat. You take a nap and sleep off the beer."

She muttered something that he didn't understand, and he left to meet up with his men.

CHAPTER FORTY-SIX

L uther had already sent the telegram by the time
Canyon arrived at the telegraph office. "Boss, I sent
out two messages. The first one went to my friend in Fort
Worth, Weldon Perry. The second one also went to Fort
Worth but to another friend by the name of Blake
Barton."

"When the replies come in, you can take the message
to Dr. Simmons's office. Brenda Wotton will get it," said
Canyon to the operator.

"Yes, sir, I know Brenda."

"Good. Now how much do I owe you for
everything?"

"That will be one dollar."

Canyon paid the man, and he and his two cowhands
went outside.

"If you want to go on to the ranch today and start
cleaning out the bunkhouse, then please do. Keep
anything you want that belonged to the previous hands.
Make a pile of everything you want to get rid of, and
we'll burn it all when Brenda and I come out tomorrow,"

said Canyon. "I figure we'll work in the house for a couple of days. At the very least, all the bedding needs washing in the bunkhouse as well as the main house."

"We'll head out directly," Luther said. "Oh, I almost forgot. There is a slop kitchen and mess hall in one of the other buildings, Do you want me to hire us a cook? Gaines fired the last one over burned biscuits and we had to cook for ourselves. A cook would sure come in handy, especially when we have trail drives and large gathers for branding."

"Sure. You're the ramrod so if you think we need one, then by all means hire one," said Canyon.

"Okay. I know of a feller here in town that might need the work and he makes some fine biscuits. We'll get our horses and stop to ask him before we go on to the Rocking G," said Luther.

"I'll be out in the morning," said Canyon.

He walked to the hotel to check on Brenda. She was still asleep, so he started lightly shaking her shoulder to wake her up. When she opened her eyes, she sat up in the bed. "What in tarnation was in that drink you gave me?"

"It was the same as mine, just a beer that you drank way too fast. How do you feel?"

"I'm fine. A little groggy, but I'm okay."

"Good. Let's go get some supper and when we're done, we'll take Isaiah a plate. I have a few items I need to discuss with you and him."

"What things?"

"We need to find out when he can leave Dr. Simmons's place, and I'd like to know a few things about his recovery."

"Oh, okay. Help me up off the bed and we can go."

A nice meal at the diner and some friendly conversation helped Brenda feel better. When she was feeling right as rain again, they took Isaiah and Club their evening meals. While Isaiah ate, Canyon and Brenda talked to the doctor.

"Doctor, when can we take Isaiah home?" asked Brenda.

He thought for a few moments and said, "I feel confident that he can leave in a couple of days if he promises not to do anything but rest so his bullet wound will heal quickly."

"What is your definition of a couple of days?" asked Canyon.

"Two at the earliest, maybe three. I recommend that you take him home in a spring-seated buggy instead of a wagon. I don't want his wound to start bleeding from the jolt of a wagon," said the doctor.

"I think a couple of days will allow us time to get his room in order and give me time to find a buggy that we can borrow," said Canyon.

"What about the men we hired? What are they doing?" asked Brenda.

"I told Luther and Gabriel that they could go on to the ranch and clear out the bunkhouse. I'm sure there're clothes and no telling what else in there."

"We'll need to do the same for the rest of the house," said Brenda.

"You and I should go there first thing in the morning so we can get started on the house," said Canyon.

"There's still plenty of daylight left. We might as well head on out there this afternoon and get a head start," said Brenda. "What do you intend to do with the stuff we don't want?"

"Throw it in the yard and burn it, I reckon," said Canyon.

"Walk with me to the hotel so I can get my things and

then we can head on out to the ranch after we tell Isaiah where we're going," said Brenda.

It only took them twenty minutes for Canyon and Brenda to collect her things and put them on their horses. They then went to see Isaiah and let him know their plans. "Brother, we're going on out to the ranch and get your room ready. We'll be back to collect you tomorrow or the next day."

"Okay, I'll be here when you get back."

Canyon went to the hurting boy and took his good hand into his. "Isaiah, you rest and do what the doctor tells you to do, and I'll be back after you. You have to know that we're all family now and you will get better."

"Thanks, Canyon."

Once they were on their horses and putting the miles behind them, Brenda spoke up. "We'll need to find a couple of big wash pots and build a fire around them. We can take the bedclothes and put them in the boiling water with some lye soap to clean them. I'm sure there's a clothesline somewhere on the property."

"I'm sure there is, but I don't remember where it is. I suspect it's behind the main house and it wouldn't surprise me if there is a building that's used as a washhouse."

"You're probably right."

When they rode into the yard, they noticed a big pile of old boots and clothes lying in the dirt between the bunkhouse and the hacienda. Canyon had started to the barn with the horses when Luther came out of the bunkhouse. "We pretty much got our quarters cleaned out. Is there something we can do to help you and Miss Brenda?"

"There is. Find some large wash pots, fill them with water and build a fire around them so she can wash the bedding."

"All that is out in the backyard. Mr. Gaines had a washroom built to do the laundry in. He was adamant about keeping his clothes and bedding clean," said Luther. "I can go ahead and get the fire going and then show it to Miss Brenda if you want me to."

"That would be great. Do you know if there is a buggy on the property?" asked Canyon.

"There sure is." Luther pointed to a barn. "That's the wagon barn, and there are wagons and buggies in there."

"Thanks, I'll go have a look." Canyon opened up the wide doors and looked at everything that was being stored. Among the various wagons and buggies, there was a two-seater carriage that would work just fine to bring Isaiah home.

While Canyon walked around the sharp-looking buggy, Gabriel came into the barn with another man.

"This is Buster Emerson. He's the new cook," said Gabriel.

"Nice to meet you, Buster. Welcome aboard," said Canyon.

"I have a stew cooking if you and the missus want to eat with us tonight," said Buster.

"We certainly will. I'm sure that Brenda will be tired by the time suppertime gets here, and won't want to cook."

Canyon finished up in the barn and went to the house to help Brenda, who was sitting in a rocker in the living room looking at a stack of papers.

"What are you looking at?" he asked.

"I think I found the papers showing that this property was part of a Spanish land grant. Here, you look at them." The yellowed papers were gathered in a worn cowhide cover, and she handed the bundle to him.

Canyon couldn't tell what they were. "You may be

right, but I think we need an expert to look them over. We'll take this with us when we go after Isaiah."

"Darling, did you happen to see my horse in the barn when you were outside?"

"Sorry, I didn't go in that barn but I'm confident that it's in there. Gaines had to have ridden it back here after leaving your house," said Canyon.

CHAPTER FORTY-SEVEN

The following two days after arriving at the Rocking G Ranch, Canyon and Brenda worked inside the main house, throwing away Paul Gaines's personal items and going through the ranch records. The bedding in the main house and for the bunkhouse was washed and hung on the clothesline to dry. Out in the yard, they made two piles of everything they didn't want to keep and sat it on fire.

Luther and Gabriel finished cleaning the bunkhouse and then started clearing out rubbish from the barns. Canyon went to the barn and stopped them from cleaning. "I have a chore for the two of you," said Canyon. "I left the wagon at the livery stable in Albany when I took Isaiah to the doctor and I'd appreciate it if you would go get it."

"Sure thing, boss. We'll get saddled up and head on out soon," said Luther.

They delivered it to the ranch and then rode out to check on the cattle and horses that were roaming on the range.

Buster made all their meals and Luther had been right —the man was a good cook.

On the third morning, Canyon harnessed a horse to the carriage and went into the house to get Brenda, who was in her bedroom combing her hair.

"Let's head out and go by the courthouse on our way into town. We'll have the judge marry us today," said Canyon.

She placed the comb on the dressing table. "Oliver, that's the smartest thing you've said in weeks. I'm ready to go."

Canyon helped her into the buggy. He looked over and there was Club sitting on the ground, watching them. "Get in, boy, you can go also. Isaiah will need company on the way home."

With the dog loaded in the back seat, they rode to Albany and stopped at the courthouse. Judge Merritt performed a simple ceremony, and they were officially married.

Canyon held his bride to his chest after they kissed. As he looked into her eyes, the past flew through his mind. The poker rooms with saloon girls and the violence of gunplay were something he wouldn't have to participate in anymore. He was happy and had the woman he wanted to spend the rest of his life with. He was blessed beyond measure. The new Canyon could now start a new exciting chapter in his life.

"Darling, what are you thinking about?" asked Brenda as she stared up at him.

"I'm just thinking how blessed I am to have you as my wife. I love you, Brenda Golden, and can't wait to spend the rest of my life with you."

She kissed him. "We should get going."

"Not yet. I need to talk to the judge."

Canyon told the judge that they were the new owners

of the Rocking G Ranch and showed him the documents they thought might be land grants.

Judge Merritt read over the papers and handed them back to Canyon. "Folks, you're the official owners of all the land in this grant. This document says that whoever has possession of it is the legal owner. So a word of advice to you: keep this in a safe place."

"Does that mean that the bank account for the ranch is also ours?" asked Canyon.

"Yes, it does. If you would like, I can notify Howard at the bank for you and give him a letter stating that you have full access of all the ranch's accounts."

"Thanks, Judge, we really appreciate your help," said Canyon, who took his bride by the arm and left.

When they were outside, Brenda pointed at a shop and said, "Let's cross over to the other side of the street. I want to go into Myrtle's store for something important."

"Okay. Do you want me to go with you or go on to Dr. Simmons's office?"

"I want you to tag along."

A middle-aged woman with her hair in a tight bun on the top of her head greeted the couple when they came through the door. "Hello folks. What can I do for you today?"

"Do you have wedding rings for sale?" asked Brenda.

"I certainly do. Follow me, please," said Myrtle.

Canyon tagged along but didn't say anything while his bride picked out whatever she wanted.

Myrtle opened a locked cabinet, removed five rings, and laid them on the countertop. Brenda picked each of them up before she went back to the first one she'd looked at. She tried it on, but it was a little too tight. "Can you make it a tiny bit bigger?" she asked.

"I certainly can." Myrtle took a tapered piece of metal

and slid the ring onto it to make it stretch out the band, then handed it back to Brenda. "Try it on now."

"It's perfect. Thank you so much," said Brenda. She removed it and turned to Canyon and handed him the ring. "Darling, put it on my finger for me, please."

He smiled a big hearty grin and took her left hand. "This ring is a token of my love for you, Brenda Golden, and may we be together until the end of the world." He slid the ring onto her finger and gave her a kiss.

Myrtle clapped her hands and sniffled with joy. "That was the sweetest thing I have ever heard in all my twenty years in business."

"Thank you so much," said Brenda. "I love my new ring. By the way, we were married right before we came here, and this is the only ring that I've ever owned."

"Congratulations on your big day. If you ever have any problems with your ring, bring it back and I'll make it right."

Canyon paid the shopkeeper, and he and Brenda headed on to see Isaiah so she could tell him the good news. When they arrived, Canyon said, "Brenda, you go on in and talk to your brother. I'll go to the telegraph office to see if we have any cowboys coming this way."

"I wish you would come in for a few minutes while I give him our good news."

"I'm sorry, you're absolutely right. We should tell him together since we're all family now."

Isaiah was sitting in a chair with his britches and boots on while the doctor was finishing up placing a new dressing on his shoulder.

"Hi, baby brother," said Brenda. "Are you able to come home today?"

"Yep, Dr. Simmons has kicked me out."

"He's recovering well and can go home with you if you have the proper transportation," said the doctor.

"We have a carriage outside," said Canyon.

"Good. I'll put a few medications together to send with you while you help the boy into his shirt. Make him use that sling over there so he won't try to use his arm too much," said the doctor, and pointed to a large piece of cloth lying on the bed.

"Okay, Doctor," said Brenda. When the doctor left the room, she took her brother's good hand in hers. "Isaiah, Canyon and I were married this morning, and he bought me this beautiful ring." She lifted her left hand to show him the ring.

Isaiah smiled and pulled his hand from hers and reached out for a hug. "I'm so proud and happy for the two of you. I already felt like we were all family, and now I know we are."

Canyon came to them and gave both Isaiah and Brenda a hug at the same time. "We are a family, and I promise to always be there for both of you. I lost my ma when I was almost nineteen and my pa a few months later. I never had any brothers or sisters and our family wasn't always the most loving. We all had our faults and one of mine was wanting to be a card shark and riverboat gambler. I love you both, and I'm committed to being the best husband and brother-in-law."

Brenda wiped a tear from her eye as Isaiah sobbed and said, "I love you both so much, and I'm ready to go home."

"Canyon, you can go on and do what business you have to do while I get Isaiah ready to travel," she added.

"Okay, I won't be long," said Canyon, and left.

Three messages were waiting for him when he arrived at the telegraph office. One was from Weldon Perry, informing Canyon that he was on his way and bringing two more cowboys. The second one was from Blake Barton, saying that he and four additional men were on their way. The third telegram was from a man by the name of Hector. All the message said was that he was on his way there.

This Hector fellow was not a name Canyon recognized from his conversation with Buster and Gabriel. He didn't know if the man was friend or foe.

Isaiah was dressed and ready to start home when Canyon returned to Dr. Simmons's office. He helped the young man into the back seat of the buggy. Club wagged his tail, happy to have his friend back.

The ride home wasn't too hard on Isaiah. Brenda had made his room ready before they'd left, and she helped him into the house and to his new bedroom. Canyon went to the bunkhouse, but no one was there. He went ahead and put the buggy back in the barn and turned the horse into the lot.

He was walking to the house when he saw three riders coming his way. Unsure of who they were, he slipped the safety thong off his gun in its holster.

The men pulled up in front of the porch where Canyon sat in a rocking chair, waiting for them. "Howdy, what can I do for you fellers?"

"Well, sir, I'm Weldon Perry and this is Dwayne." He pointed to his right. "The other feller goes by Dogger. We're supposed to have jobs here."

"I'm Oliver Canyon Golden, and you can call me Canyon. I own this place along with my wife. The job pays thirty a month. We have a really good cook, and the bunkhouse is that long building to the north. Luther Albertson is the ranch foreman and he should be back later. You men can go ahead and stow your things and go over to the mess hall to eat if you want."

"Much obliged," said Weldon.

The men were turning their horses to leave when

Canyon said, "Hold up a second. Have any of you ever heard of a man that goes by Hector?"

"Yeah, he's a hired gun. He sells out to the man with the most money. If you are hiring him, then we'll be moving on," said Weldon.

"Nope, I ain't hiring him or any hired guns. But it seems like he's on his way here for me. Don't let that bother the three of you, though. I'll take care of Hector. He's my problem if he comes here."

Canyon's eye caught on a cloud of dust off to the south and pointed that way so the others could see. "It looks like Luther and Gabriel are coming back. You fellers get settled in and we'll talk more over supper."

CHAPTER FORTY-EIGHT

Four weeks had passed since Canyon and Brenda had married and moved into the hacienda at the Rocking G Ranch. Luther was able to hire a total of twelve cowhands to help with the cattle operation. Isaiah was much better, but Brenda wouldn't let him go off with the others until he was totally healed.

The cowhands had been spending most days on the range with the cattle. One morning, Luther came to the house so he could talk to Canyon about ranch business. Canyon met him on the porch and invited him inside the house where it was cooler.

"Luther, have a seat and tell me what I can do for you."

Luther sat on the divan with his hat in his hand. "We've been looking the herd over for the past few weeks, and I think it's time to drive some cattle to market. Fall will be here soon, and then winter. We sure don't need to feed the number of cattle that I've been seeing," said Luther.

"Okay. When do you plan on doing that, and where do you think we need to take them?" asked Canyon.

"We should spend next week separating out the old cows and bigger steers. Then we can leave here and drive them to Abilene. I figure it will take us four days to get there if everything goes smoothly," said Luther.

"Do you have any idea how many head we'll have to take to market?"

"I'm thinking somewhere between 1,500 and 2,000 head. That's a lot of cattle, so you might want to go into Albany and send a telegram to the buyer so he can be prepared."

"That's a good idea. I'll go there today," said Canyon. He got up and started to pace, deep in thought. "We'll need to let Buster know so he can have the wagon stocked with trail grub. Do you think we have enough hands to make the cattle drive on our own, or do we need to hire a few more?"

"I can't say right offhand because I don't know how many head we have right now. The number of cattle will dictate how much help we need. I believe that if you, Brenda, and Isaiah all go, then we would probably have enough."

"I certainly can go, but I don't want Brenda to go. As for Isaiah, we'll see if he's really needed. One other thing, I'm going to leave it up to you to make sure we have everything we need. I helped Brenda's grandpa once drive a few head to Abilene, but I'm no cowboy."

"I can take care of everything, boss. I've already assigned three men the task of rounding up the horse herd and driving them to the corral. We'll have a remuda to take with us so we can change out to fresh mounts during the day."

"Good. Let's get our plan in motion. I'll go into town and send a telegram to the buyer," said Canyon, and stood up to shake hands with his foreman.

After Luther left, Brenda came into the room. "What did Luther want?"

Canyon explained the plan of driving cattle to Abilene and that he needed to go into Albany to send out a telegram.

"Are you going to ride into town with me?" he asked.

"Sure. If you don't mind, could we take the carriage so I can bring a few things back with me?"

"Of course. I'll go get it and meet you out front in twenty minutes," said Canyon.

The ride was a pleasant one, and Canyon parked the buggy in front of the dress shop next to the mercantile.

"Honey, you take as long as you like and buy whatever you want. I'm going to the telegraph office and then to the saloon to have a beer. If I ain't back by the time you finish up, you know where I'll be. Who knows, you may want a mug before we head home."

"Oliver Golden, I can't believe you would say such a thing to a lady," said Brenda. She smiled at him as she walked into the dress shop.

Canyon sent the telegram to the cattle buyer in Abilene that Bart had used when they took cattle to market, giving them notice of his intentions. He left the office and stopped in at the leather goods shop and bought himself a new vest. As he was coming out of the store, the telegraph operator flagged him down, waving a piece of paper in the air.

"Your reply came back mighty fast, Canyon."

"Yes it did. Thanks for bringing it to me."

The telegram informed Canyon that the buyer would take all the cattle he wanted to sell, and pay nine dollars a head. That was fine with Canyon, especially since he could make a lot of money without having to gamble for it.

After securing the piece of paper in his shirt pocket,

Canyon walked to the saloon and entered without giving his eyes time to adjust to the dim lighting. That was something he always did and the mistake caused him to almost trip on the leg of a chair before he stopped and let his eyes regulate. Two poker tables had games going and most of the men in the room he had seen in town before, except for a slick-looking man sporting a goatee and wearing a nice black hat and red shirt.

Canyon bellied up to the bar and the barkeep brought him a mug of beer. He took a big swallow while watching the stranger in the mirror.

One of the tables only had three players. Canyon recognized them—the man who owned the hardware store, and two local cowhands.

The hardware owner spoke up. "Oliver, do you want to join us for a few hands?"

The stranger Canyon had been watching jerked his head up, and with his right hand reached down to remove the safety from his gun.

Without taking his eyes off the stranger, Canyon said, "No, I'm not playing poker anymore. There comes a time when a feller has to know when to fold and move on. But thanks for asking."

Canyon picked up his beer with his left hand. He slid his right hand under his vest and removed the gun from his shoulder holster, but kept both hand and gun hidden.

The stranger walked toward Canyon, stopping ten feet away. "My name is Hector Gaines, and I've come to kill you. Turn around real slow, and we'll end this today."

Canyon took another swallow of his beer and put the empty mug on the bar. With his back to the man, he said, "Hector, I've already killed your nephew and your brother. What makes you think that you have a chance against me?"

"I'm much faster than they were. Turn around."

Canyon pushed the mug to his left and started to turn. He still had his right hand concealed in his vest. "It looks like this is going to be the place where you die," he said, and pulled the gun and fired at the gunslinger. Hector never got a shot off and lay dead in a pool of blood.

Canyon flipped a half dollar onto the bar and started to the door. Another gamble that hadn't gone well for his opponent.

CHAPTER FORTY-NINE

One week after Canyon shot and killed Hector Gaines, the cattle drive to Abilene was about to get started. Luther had herded the cows they would be selling to the range north of the hacienda, where they waited to be driven to market.

The sun was coming up in the east, and Luther fired his gun so everyone would know it was time to get started. Canyon, Club, Isaiah, and twelve other men were gathered to listen to the foreman give them instructions.

Luther said, "Canyon will ride point. Weldon, Gabriel, and Blake will ride drag. Billy and Isaiah will lead the remuda and the rest of us will be outriders. Today will be our hardest day, so be sure to change horses when you need to. Buster, you head on out with the wagon, but keep it to the side of the drive in case the herd stampedes."

The riders mounted up and spread out as they came up on the herd of cattle grazing on the short dried-out bluestem grass. All the men worked together, whooping and hitting the backs of the animals to get the herd started.

Once they were going in the right direction, Canyon and Club moved to the front of the herd. The beasts were massive, with horns that could go right through man and horse. It was a dangerous place to be, but Canyon felt it was his responsibility to lead the way. He picked out a bull that looked larger and older than the rest and made him the leader of the herd. An old, strong bull that had been with the herd for some time seemed to be a leader, and the cows and younger bull would generally follow him.

By noon the horses were tired, and the men had changed to fresh mounts. But the cows had finally gotten in step with the old bull and had taken to the trail behind him.

They were only able to travel ten miles that first day before the men stopped for supper and rest. The swing riders kept busy going after cows that wanted to leave the herd before the cows finally settled down as it started to get dark. By the time they bedded down for the night, both the men and their horses were tired.

After supper that first night, Luther assigned teams to ride nighthawks and keep the herd bunched. The night riders rode circles around the cattle singing to them. That seemed to help keep them settled down just knowing that riders were out there.

The second day they were able to make it twelve miles, but the cows were beginning to bellow in need of water.

"Men, you'll have to watch the herd closer tonight," said Luther that night. "They're thirsty, and so are the horses."

"I know of a large tank that's big enough for all our animals to take on water," said Canyon. "I'm pretty sure we can make it there tomorrow."

"Okay. We'll have an early breakfast in the morning

so we can get them back on the trail. The quicker we start, the better," said Luther. "Everyone needs to know that when those cows smell water, they'll pick up their pace. Don't get in their way, or they'll run over you. When the first bunch gets a drink, you cowboys will have to move them on out or they will stay in the water."

"Maybe we could divide the herd in thirds and get the first ones started at daylight and then the second bunch an hour later," said Canyon.

"I've never seen that done before, but it might work. We'll all pitch in on the first group and get them moving, and then only five of you will have to take them on to the water hole," said Luther.

That next morning, the hands divided the herd and got the first ones heading north. They had gone about three miles when the lead bull smelled water and just as Luther had predicted, he walked a little faster. Five riders, along with the dog, stayed with the first group while the other cowboys went after the second bunch.

The wranglers that were with the first set of longhorns had just got the cattle on the trail again when they saw more cattle coming their way. The dog had helped in a great way, nipping at the back legs of the cows to make them go. He was getting their attention every time the ones at the rear slowed down or tried to leave the herd. Club would run at them, and if they didn't turn back, he would bite their legs. It didn't take long before he had his way and they ran from him.

Canyon, who was with the lead head of cattle, gave his men their next assignment. "Three of us will move this first group to some good graze, and two of you go back and help the others."

Three hours later, the entire herd had been watered and were much easier to trail. That night went without a hitch, and everyone was in the saddle at daylight the next morning.

Once the cattle were lined out along the trail, Canyon went to find Luther. "I'm certain that we can make Abilene tomorrow. Do you suspect the cattle will give us any problems tonight?"

"I don't think so. The water stop did them good, and if we stop on some good graze, they will get some moisture from the grass. I do think we should get started at daylight again tomorrow. Boss man, do you know how to get to the shipping pens once we get there?" asked Luther.

"I do. I've been here once before with Brenda, Isaiah, and their grandpa. I'm hoping that old lead bull will follow me into the pens and never look back."

At eleven o'clock the morning of the fourth day on the trail drive, the herd made it into pens, which were situated along the railroad tracks. By two in the afternoon all the cattle were enclosed along the tracks, ready to be loaded onto railcars. They were able to put the horse remuda in one of the pastures where there was water and grass for them to eat.

Canyon got his check for the herd and came outside of the buyer's office. His men sat resting in the shade while waiting on him. "Men, you all did a fine job on this cattle drive. I have to stop by the bank to cash the check for the cows. I'll meet you all at the saloon so we can wash the trail dust from our throats. Then we can eat and head home. I figure we can get ten miles behind us before it gets too dark."

Buster stood up from where he sat on the wagon tongue to speak. "Boss man, I don't drink, so iffin it's all right with you, I'll take the wagon and head on back. When I find a good place to camp for the night, I'll go ahead and set up for breakfast in the morning."

"Buster, that's a good idea. We'll see you later tonight," said Canyon. He looked at his dog, resting in the shade. "Club, you get in the wagon with Buster, and keep him company until we get there later tonight." The dog took a few steps toward the wagon and then looked back at Canyon. "Go on, boy," Canyon said. "You deserve some rest also."

At the saloon, Canyon and the dusty cowboys from the cattle drive filled up three tables, and a few stood at the bar too. He told the bartender to give his men whatever they wanted, and he would pay. Then he asked, "Why is the place so empty? Usually it's busy in here this time of day."

"There's some sickness going around, and most folks are staying home. It's been that way for a couple of weeks now," said the bartender.

They all had a few drinks, and then Canyon and Luther made everyone go to the café. The dining room was empty, so they had the whole place to themselves. After a good meal, they mounted up and headed to get the horses they had in the meadow by the cattle pens. The horses were used to them and didn't give the cowboys any problems as they headed out of town to find Buster.

It didn't take them but two hours to find the wagon with Buster and Club already asleep under the wagon.

The following morning the sky was overcast, and there was a hint of rain in the air. Canyon and his crew headed out at a good pace. They could afford to travel faster than usual, since they had the remuda of horses with them.

Around three that afternoon, Canyon began to cough and feel bad with fatigue and body aches. He hardly touched his food that evening and by breakfast time the next morning, he was feverish and coughing even more and spitting up phlegm. His dog wouldn't leave his side, as if nervous about his master's health.

Luther came over and said, "I'm assigning two of the men to take extra horses to get you home faster. Do you think you can ride?"

"Yeah, I can ride. Let's get going," said Canyon. "Club, you stay with Buster, and I'll see you at home."

By early afternoon he was so feverish that he didn't know if he could ride anymore. Jacob, one of the cowboys who was accompanying him, said, "Billy, you change your horse out for a fresh one and ride as hard as you can to the ranch and bring the buggy back. Tell Miss Brenda to ride into Albany and get the doctor."

They helped Canyon off his horse and laid him on the ground under a tree where there was shade. Billy changed to a fresh mount and headed out. Jacob helped Canyon back into the saddle and rode along beside him, holding on to his arm so he wouldn't fall off his horse. Canyon coughed and wheezed and was covered in sweat.

Billy had the buggy to them by six o'clock along with a fresh horse that they swapped out to pull the carriage back.

By the time the two cowhands arrived at the ranch with Canyon, Dr. Simmons was waiting on them. Canyon was so weak that Jacob and Billy had to guide him into the house and help get him into bed.

Brenda wiped his face and chest with a cool, damp washcloth. His coughing was so bad that he motioned for them to sit him up in hopes it would help clear out his lungs.

Dr. Simmons gave him a big swallow of laudanum. "Canyon, when did you start feeling sick?"

With a weak voice, he said, "Yesterday, after we left Abilene."

"Were you around anyone who was coughing or running fever?"

"Not that I know of."

"I'm really sorry to tell you this, but tuberculosis is infecting people in Abilene. I'm afraid you've caught it, and there is nothing I can do for you. It infects the lungs, and people have to ride it out. If they can."

Brenda looked at the doctor with tears running down her cheeks. "Are you telling me that my husband is dying?"

"No, I'm telling you that he has a fighting chance of beating it. You and everyone else who comes in contact with him ought to wear a handkerchief over your mouth and nose. Some folks call it the consumption, and there is no cure for it yet. Keep giving him the laudanum and hot toddies for the cough. I've done all I can do tonight, but I'll be back tomorrow."

CHAPTER FIFTY

B renda sat with her husband all night, putting cold rags on his face, neck, and arms to help with the fever. His breathing was labored, and he wheezed so badly he could hardly talk. About daylight, Brenda heard Club barking at the back door. She tried to ignore him, but the noise woke up Isaiah, who let him in the house.

The dog ran to Canyon's bedroom and put his front paws on the bed. Canyon moved his hand closer, and the dog started to lick it.

Brenda put a hand to her husband's forehead. "Canyon, I'm sending Isaiah into Albany to have the doctor come back out. I also want the preacher to come here and pray over you."

He reached out to his wife and pulled her close so she could hear him. "I've done a lot of bad things in my life." He had to stop to get more air before he could continue. "I made peace with God after I killed Paul Gaines." He started coughing and struggled for breath. "I repented for my sins and started trusting Jesus that day."

"I'm so proud of you. I love you so much, Canyon.

But we need the doctor here now. I hope he can do something more for you."

Canyon smiled and squeezed her hand. "I love you, my darling."

"I love you too." Brenda got off the bed. "Come with me, Club."

The dog barked and growled at her. "You don't growl at me. I'll take a broom to you. Now get up and go outside."

"Brenda, let him stay. I'm mighty thirsty. Will you get me a cool glass of water?"

"Of course I will. First, let me send Isaiah after the doctor." She left the room.

"Come up here, old friend." Canyon patted the blanket and his dog got up on the bed with him.

Canyon rubbed Club's head, and in a whisper, he said, "Boy, this time I haven't seen the death angel dressed in black ready to take me home. I'm going to be all right, you just wait and see."

Brenda stepped into the room. "I heard what you told Club, and you had better be telling the truth, because I'm pregnant."

A LOOK AT: CARD, KILL THEM ALL

(CARD JORDAN 1)

Step into a pulse-pounding western adventure where justice rides on a bullet and vengeance blazes a trail across the untamed frontier.

In 1875, sixteen-year-old Card Jordan returns from his first solo hunting trip to discover a nightmare—his family brutally murdered by a ruthless gang. Scrawled in the dirt beside his mother's body are the words that will forever change his destiny: CARD, KILL THEM ALL.

Fueled by vengeance and armed with his father's Cavalry hat, Card plunges headlong into a relentless western adventure. He must leave his innocence behind and become a force for frontier justice, tracking the killers through the wilds of North Texas and Indian Territory. Along the way, Card endures heartbreak, illness, and the unforgiving challenges of the Old West, sharpening his skills as a gunfighter with every step.

As Card closes in on the gang's vicious leader, Ned Black, his quest for retribution becomes a test of courage, resolve, and the true meaning of justice. Will avenging his family bring him peace—or only more pain?

Don't miss *Card, Kill Them All*—the explosive first book in the Card Jordan series. If you crave classic western adventures packed with danger, grit, and high-stakes action, saddle up and start reading today!

AVAILABLE NOW

ABOUT THE AUTHOR

Monty was born and raised in Southeastern Oklahoma in the small town of Sawyer, which is nested along the banks of the Kiamichi River. He's owned horses and cattle, riding the former and working the latter. Over the years, he formed a deep connection and respect for the Old West and the courageous folks who braved the wild frontier.

Monty is an avid reader and is particularly enthusiastic when it comes to Western authors and novels. His love of reading sparked his desire to write his first short story. He loves writing about real places and landmarks from the 1800s. In college, he wrote a ten-page paper about his grandmother, born in 1886, who married at fourteen and took in five orphaned nieces and nephews shortly thereafter. Monty's love for history and penchant for storytelling earned him an A+, and he hasn't looked back since.

Now retired, he loves to travel, fish, spend time with his four grandkids, and tell stories. He looks for inspiration for future books wherever he goes, and he is a member of the Western Writers of America Inc.

www.montygarnerauthor.com